THE FUNNIEST BOY IN THE WORLD

Helen Rutter

SCHOLASTIC

Published in the UK by Scholastic, 2023
1 London Bridge, London, SE1 9BG
Scholastic Ireland, 89E Lagan Road, Dublin Industrial Estate, Glasnevin,
Dublin, D11 HP5F

SCHOLASTIC and associated logos are trademarks and/or
registered trademarks of Scholastic Inc.

ISBN 978 0702 31467 4

A CIP catalogue record for this book
is available from the British Library.

Printed by CPI Group (UK) Ltd, Croydon, CR0 4YY
Paper made from wood grown in sustainable forests
and other controlled sources.

1 3 5 7 9 10 8 6 4 2

www.scholastic.co.uk

THE FUNNIEST BOY IN THE WORLD
is Helen's third novel. Helen's first book,
THE BOY WHO MADE EVERYONE LAUGH,
was one of the bestselling debuts of 2020, and
shortlisted for the Costa Children's Book Award,
the Blue Peter Best Story Book, the Branford
Boase Award, among many other prizes. Her
second book, THE BOY WHOSE WISHES CAME
TRUE, was chosen as a Sunday Times and Times
Children's Book of the Week. Helen lives just
outside Sheffield and has worked as an actress
for many years. The idea for her stories starring
Billy Plimpton came from her son, Lenny, who
has a stammer: she wanted to write a book that
he would love to read, starring a child like him.

OTHER BOOKS BY HELEN RUTTER

The Boy Who Made Everyone Laugh
The Boy Whose Wishes Came True

To the sixty seventh Rob.
The funniest boy in my world.

CHAPTER 1

What happened when the tiger ate the comedian?

He felt funny.

I close my eyes and I'm right there again, looking out at all the laughing faces; people are cheering, shouting my name, tears streaming down their cheeks. I can feel the velvet curtains and hear the rustle of sweet packets and the applause. The applause was the best part. The part that made my head go buzzy and my face go numb and my hands get pins and needles. That's what I want again. APPLAUSE. It's like I NEED it. Everyone needs air and water to live – I also need laughter.

I dream about the end-of-term talent show at least

once a week, even though it was months ago now. I always feel amazing the morning after one of those dreams. I get up whistling and don't even try and wind my little sister Chloe up at breakfast by building a wall of cereal boxes between us and telling her ponies are evil.

Unfortunately, I didn't have the talent show dream last night. Therefore, the wall of cereal was firmly in place at breakfast, in spite of Chloe's moaning on the other side of the Weetabix.

Last night's dream was bad: it was about the baby again. This time the baby was massive and chasing me through a dark forest with a dummy in its mouth.

The baby's not even here yet, and it's already annoying. It makes Mum cry all the time. I walked into the living room yesterday and she was blubbing over a property programme. How two couples choosing a really expensive house can make you cry, I don't know.

"Sorry, love, I'm hormonal – it's the baby," she said, patting her massive bump, as if that explained it all. That's what she says every time she cries or shouts or has a massive laughing fit and nearly pees her pants.

"It's the baby."

She's at it again now. I'm helping her paint the

baby's room and I can see the tears rolling down her cheeks as we put yet another coat of yellow paint on the walls. Who knows what set her off this time?

The only reason I'm helping is because she said she would give me a fiver, and I knew she'd cry if I said no. It started off quite fun; we played really loud music and she let me paint my name on the wall. Then I did a mural of us all, but when I painted Mum I did her as a massive beach ball with a tiny head. I thought it was funny, but she got annoyed and turned the music down. Now we're on our third coat and there's no music at all. It's really boring and a fiver is not worth it.

I could be earning my own money if Mum and Dad would just let me do some comedy gigs. I could be famous by now. I could have bought them the stupid yellow paint and even paid a decorator to put it on the walls. They don't understand that I should be building my comedy career, not covering my face in splashes of "Pantofle Yellow".

"Pantofle" is a stupid name for paint, if you ask me. When Mum and Dad were choosing the colour, all the paints had ridiculous names like "Baboon's Breath" and "Pale Dog" – who comes up with these things? Baboon's breath is obviously see-through like anyone else's breath, although apparently, according to the fancy paint company, it is paler than "Shrew's Breath" – yet another daft colour. What kind of pale dog are they talking about? It makes no sense. "Pale Brown Dog" I would understand but just "Pale Dog" is meaningless.

I asked Mum what a Pantofle was, and she didn't know so I googled it. It's a slipper, for goodness' sake, and not even a yellow slipper. I think the paint people are having a laugh, seeing what they can get away with. Like when Harry Wilson put the word anchovy in his English homework five times to see if the teacher would notice. They didn't. He got a smiley face stamp and two green ticks, which makes me wonder if any of the teachers ever read any of our homework.

I wrote a list of the most stupid paint names I could find and stuck it up on my pinboard. Here are my current top three:

STUPID PAINT NAMES

1. Cabbage Brown. Last time I checked, cabbage definitely *was not brown*. Unless it's gone bad. Who would want a rotten vegetable on their walls?

2. Dead Cod. I sincerely hope that no fish were harmed in the making of this paint.
3. Barbara's Blushes. Who is Barbara, and what on earth has she done?

Another splash of paint flicks off the brush and hits my nose. This is such a waste of time. I should be performing, not painting!

After the talent show and the news interview, I was offered loads of stuff: gigs in real-life comedy clubs and slots on TV and everything, but before I could say yes, Mum and Dad insisted we all "discuss this properly".

I always know it's going to be bad when they say we have to discuss something properly. It means they're definitely going to say no, we just have to talk about it a lot first. The time they wouldn't let me have a telly in my room; the time I was not allowed to go to Laser Quest with Alex because it was in a "dodgy" bit of town; the time I HAD to do our "traditional" Easter egg hunt with Chloe instead of just getting cash from the Easter Bunny. All of those were "discussed properly" first and the answer was no for every single one.

The discussion about my gigs went the same way.

"We have talked about this, Billy, but as it's still your first year of secondary school, we think you should focus on that. You can't miss school for interviews or be staying up late for gigs, it's not sensible."

"B-B-B-Being a comedian *isn't* sensible, though, is it? The clue's in the n-n-name, Mum ... comedian. As in, someone who makes people laugh, n-n-not someone who is sensible."

"You are a twelve-year-old schoolboy, Billy. Not a comedian."

"I'm a twelve-year-old schoolboy *comedian*! That's my hook, my USP, my thing. That's why those journalists and gig bookers want me! I need to strike now, b-b-build my brand."

"Well, you can 'build your brand' all you like in the summer holidays. Until then, you are an ordinary schoolboy."

"B-B-But—"

"That's the end of it, Billy. We are not getting into one of your debates over this. We love that you have found your confidence. You can do all the school plays and talent shows at Bannerdale that you want. The other stuff will have to wait. It's only a few months."

My parents didn't get it. They thought that

prancing around the stage in the drama club summer show is the same as being a comedian, but it's not. As if I would be seen dead doing a stupid dance routine from *Grease*! I wanted more than school shows. I wanted to be a proper comedian on a real stage.

I couldn't change their mind, though. I've spent a few boring months waiting – but finally my summer of real-life comedy is nearly here. And I'm going to start it with a bang. In just under two weeks, I'm going to do my first proper stand-up gig.

It all started when I walked past the King's Head last week on my way back from seeing Mrs Gibbens, an old lady I visit at her care home. I'd never really noticed the pub before, apart from having to step around people smoking outside or bottles on the pavement. Someone was up a ladder, putting up a huge sign. People say you need to look out for signs in life to tell you what to do. Well, this was an actual sign!

COMEDY NIGHT

First Friday of every month.

I emailed them straight away. I told them that I don't even need to be paid; I'm happy to do it for free until I'm famous. I need the practice. I got an email back the same night, offering me an "open spot". I looked it up. An open spot means doing a short stand-up slot for free.

They had watched the clips that I'd sent from the talent show and the news interview and said they would love for me to come and perform! Apparently, kids aren't allowed in the pub after nine p.m., though, so I am going onstage first and then will go straight home. I also have to be with an adult so Dad's taking me. There's no way that Mum would come. She's usually in bed by nine anyway: "It's the baby."

At first Mum and Dad, of course, said no.

"There is no way you are hanging around in that grotty pub, Billy."

But I was not going to let them get away with ruining my comedy career for a second longer. I knew that this gig was the best way to start my summer of stand-up. Besides, we break up for the holidays in a month so they can't use the education excuse any more. I wrote the best persuasive letter that I could:

Dear Mum and Dad,

As you know, it has long been my dream to be a professional stand-up comedian. I have put in the work, dedication and commitment that I believe it takes to make it. I have risen to the challenges and dealt with the turmoil of standing onstage with a stammer. You helped me get to where I am today, but now is the time to let me spread my wings and fly into the world of comedy.

The gig is on Friday night -- NOT a school night. I will be finished by nine p.m., so I will lose no sleep and it will not impact on my schooling. Also -- Dad, you will get a night out at the pub!

It will be a great way to start my summer of flexing my muscles in the comedy world, it will build my confidence, and if you don't let me, I will be miserable and impossible to live with -- FOR EVER.

So please, please, please, please,

please, please, please, please, please,
please, please, please, with a cherry
on top, say yes.
I love you so much,
Your gorgeous, cute, inspiring,
amazing and hilarious son

Obviously they then said yes! I can't wait. The crowd, the laughter, the applause: it will all be mine!

A blob of paint drips from my brush on to my bare foot, bringing me back to reality. Mum sighs, puts her brush down and waddles out of the room for her fifth wee in the last hour – I'm counting. Apparently, as well as turning you into an emotional wreck, babies also make you wee your pants.

I look into the mirror, which is leaning against the cot, and go back to imagining my first gig of the summer. I lift the paintbrush towards my mouth.

"Hello, ladies and gentlemen. G-G-Good evening, everyone. Please welcome to the stage the one and only, the best – the only – schoolboy comedian the world has ever seen … B-B-Billy Plimpton!"

I close my eyes. The crowded room is full and the audience is hanging on my every word. Tears of joy stream down faces; people hold their sides, they are laughing so hard; they chant my name. I need to be escorted from the pub by bouncers to protect me from my adoring fans, their hands stretching out to reach me.

I have read the email about a thousand times. I know it off by heart. It said that the room seats up to a hundred people (that's a lot of people!). I have to do exactly ten minutes and they will flash a light at me to tell me when I have one minute left. I've been practising my set every day. It's exactly ten minutes long. All my favourite jokes are in there and a couple of impressions too. Here are my current top three jokes:

TOP THREE JOKES

1. When someone tells me to stop acting like a flamingo, that's when I put my foot down.
2. Why do birds have feathers? To cover up their butt quack.
3. I said to my PE teacher, "Can you teach me to do the splits?" He said, "How flexible are you?" I said, "I can't do Tuesdays."

I've never actually been inside the King's Head pub before, so I have to do a lot of imagining. There is a chance that in my head the stage is fancier, the audience is bigger and the laughter is louder. I *could* be slightly exaggerating what will actually be a pretty ordinary pub. But you never know, there *could* be adoring fans.

This gig *could* make me famous – couldn't it?

CHAPTER 2

Why did the egg get thrown out of class?

Because it kept telling yolks.

On Monday at school, while Mr Osho is taking the register, Skyla arrives. She's late again. She wasn't in at all for three days last week, and before that she was arriving later and later every day. Skyla's always been a bit like that. Even when we were in primary she would come in late, wearing dirty uniform or looking like she'd just got out of bed, but recently it's got worse. At primary I didn't really think about it. We weren't friends back then, and I was too busy worrying about my stammer. But now I've started to notice the ways that she's different to everyone else.

Skyla is a bit like a wild animal being forced into

a uniform and told to behave like the rest of us. But she's not like the rest of us. Her life is different. It's weird how adults expect all kids to behave the same, look the same and care about the same things, when we go home to completely different lives.

I tried calling Skyla yesterday to find out what was going on, but she didn't answer, and she hasn't replied to any of my texts. When things are bad at home, she vanishes. She's never told me what's actually going on. All I know is, since her baby sister died, her mum hasn't been the same. That was years ago, so it's been bad for ages. I asked her about it once and she told me to "Stop being such a Debbie Downer". And then she punched me on the arm and skipped off down the corridor. I didn't ask again.

"Come on in, Skyla," Mr Osho says with a smile. "Are you feeling better?"

"Yes, sir," she mumbles, but it's obvious something's not right. When she goes to sit down, I try to catch her eye, but she keeps her head down, eyes on the floor.

"What's going on with her?" Alex whispers.

"No idea."

Our first lesson is history. We all walk into the class reluctantly. We have a new teacher – Mr

Johnson – and he's horrible. My friends, The Regulars, started calling him Shouty Man and now the whole of Year Seven call him that too. I'm glad I've got Alex, Josh and Matthew around me. Whenever Shouty Man is telling someone off we all make funny faces to make each other laugh. I hope he never catches us.

Shouty Man sent Josh out for jiggling the other day, before we'd even sat down. Then, when he was allowed back in he started jiggling again, which is just what Josh does, and Shouty Man sent him out again! It was totally unfair. He has given me three negatives for tapping too. One more and I'll get a detention.

The reason I tap so much is because he terrifies me. The tapping calms me down. It doesn't help with my stammer, though. My stammer is SO bad in Mr Johnson's lessons, even though I've got The Regulars by my side. I'm glad we didn't have him when I first started at Bannerdale, when I had no friends and was still hiding under the stairwell. Back then, Mr Johnson would probably have made me wet myself.

Shouty Man is the only teacher who gives out negatives. Most of the others threaten them but never follow it through. We have to carry a little pink card around with us and it has four spaces for negatives. When it gets full you get an automatic detention. Caleb McCraven in Year Nine sells fake ones for a quid so you can always have an empty card and dodge detention.

I'm too scared to talk to Caleb McCraven, though. He has a scar on his face and once head-butted someone in a fight at the gates. Which means I have three negatives on my card and I can't get another one before the summer holidays. Mum and Dad would not be pleased if I got a detention. They might even say I can't do my stand-up gig, which would be a total disaster.

I've seen Shouty Man prowling the halls at lunchtime and giving out negatives for wonky ties and mismatched socks. I'm really trying not to tap in history now. I sit on my hands, although he might give me a negative for that too. A detention for tapping or hand-sitting both seem a bit over the top to me, but clearly not to Shouty Man. He barks instead of speaking: "In my class, you will not fiddle, wriggle, whisper, stare out of the window, pick your nose, swing your feet or crack your knuckles. DO NOT pick up your pen, or anything else for that matter, until I specifically ask you to do so. Understand?"

Even when Shouty Man is talking about history, he barks. It's pretty impressive how he can make the Norman Conquest sound like a direct threat. It's as though he's literally going to send us all into battle if we so much as think about touching our pencil cases. Blakemore thinks he's ex-military.

"I can always spot 'em," he says. "My dad used to be in the army; he's the same, loves rules … and shouting."

Today, as I'm struggling not to pick off the splashes of Pantofle Yellow from my fingers, Mr Johnson is shouting at us about Anne Boleyn. She had a bad enough time of it, what with being beheaded. I'm sure she would not want the details of her life being spat out angrily at a bunch of mildly terrified twelve-year-olds.

"She was beheaded on the 19th of May 1536 at the Tower of London. Skyla Norkins, are you listening to me? Do not EVER close your eyes in my class."

Everyone looks at Skyla, who has gone really pale. Then, before Mr Johnson can shout or give out a thousand negatives, she collapses.

Her body slumps into her chair and her head lolls forward, banging hard on the desk. It looks like she's been shot. Yasmin is sitting next to her and screams but manages to grab her before she slides on to the floor. I get up to help, but Mr Johnson shouts, "DOWN." I immediately sit back in my chair like a scared puppy in a training class.

We all stare. This feels different to the usual classroom dramas. Different to when Raya Fletcher vomited in the science lab and stank out the whole room (the corner by the Bunsen burners still smells like sick). Different to when Elijah Campbell's chair broke and he fell head first on to the floor. Different to when Elliot Baker tied Arik Weber's shoelaces together in food tech and he tripped and fell into a lasagne. Everyone is really freaked out.

But Mr Johnson is totally calm – maybe Blakemore is right and he *is* ex-military. He tells Yasmin to go and get the nurse and then he asks Sonny to move his table and chair away to make space. Then he puts Skyla on the floor in the recovery position, stands up and says, in the quietest voice I have ever heard him use, "Everyone gather your things in total silence and go to the library. I expect you all to have written one side of A4 on Henry VIII's wives by the next lesson. You are dismissed."

It's like magic. We do exactly as he says and, ten

minutes later, we are sitting in the library slightly stunned.

I keep picturing Skyla flopping over on to her desk, again and again. Then, out of nowhere, another image pops into my brain. The Oaks care home. The day Granny Bread died. It's like I'm there again, the day it happened. Walking up the corridor to her little room. Heart thumping in my chest, outside of myself, knowing that my life is about to change.

Sometimes that memory pops up in my brain like a horrible surprise.

After Granny Bread died I couldn't walk up that corridor in The Oaks for a long time. The first time I took Scraggles the dog to see Mrs Gibbens was the worst. Looking at Mrs Gibbens's door and then further down to the closed door of Granny Bread's room, knowing that someone else would be inside now. I saw it and couldn't breathe. Scraggles sat on my feet, as though he knew. It felt like Mum was going to appear and tell me Granny Bread had died all over again. I would have to relive the whole thing. Mum said it was like PTSD, which stands for POST TRAUMATIC STRESS DISORDER. It means that sometimes, when something bad happens, your brain remembers it over and over.

I feel a bit like that now. My brain keeps replaying Skyla slumping down, the sound of her head hitting the desk. What if this is like that day in The Oaks? One minute Granny Bread was here and the next she'd vanished. What if Skyla has vanished too? What if there is something wrong with her and I don't even know because I stopped asking her what was going on? I shouldn't have stopped. I should have kept trying, even if she punches me on the arm and tells me to shut up.

I don't write a single word about Henry VIII or his wives. I sit and stare at the blank page and count my breaths up to ten and then start again, like Mum taught me, until the bell goes.

At break I run straight to the medical room and Skyla is sitting on the chair outside, holding a biscuit and some orange juice. She hasn't vanished, but she still doesn't look fully here.

"W-What happened?"

"I fainted, that's all. Everyone's making such a big deal about it."

"But w-why did you faint? It was pretty dramatic. Mr J-Johnson even stopped shouting."

"No way!"

"Yup, who knew you had that much power?"

We laugh and I feel so relieved that she's all right that I almost don't ask the question. But I know I need to. It's important.

"So, w-what's g-g-going on, Skyla?"

"I'm tired and I forgot to have breakfast," she says, breezily.

"You've not been in for d-d-days."

"Who are you, the attendance police?!"

She snorts. I feel really frustrated. This is what Skyla does. She makes it impossible to find out anything. She's always been there for me. When Blakemore used to bully me, she never ignored it, or laughed it off. I want to look after her like she's looked after me. But if she won't tell me what's going on, I don't know how to.

The school nurse comes out of the medical room. I hate the smell in there – like chemicals. I once had to go when Matthew accidentally trod on my finger and we thought it was broken. The smell was so bad it made my finger stop hurting immediately. Maybe that's the idea; make it so stinky that everyone says they're feeling better just so they can leave.

"Your mum isn't answering, Skyla," the nurse says. "I can't see another number on your form. Is there anyone else I can call?"

"No. I'm fine. I'll go back to lessons."

"Well, eat your biscuit and drink your juice. I'll keep trying your mum."

"She won't answer today," Skyla says quietly.

"Is she at work?"

"No, she's … busy."

I can tell that Skyla won't say any more. The nurse sighs and goes back into her room.

Skyla takes a sip of her juice and then kind of shakes her head, breathes in and smiles at me. "I finished the projections for your gig." I know her smile is fake bright now, but if this is what she needs, I'm always happy to talk about my gig.

Skyla's done some animations to have up on a screen behind me as I do my set. It's going to be so cool; she's drawn cartoon versions of me to go with some of my jokes.

"Amazing, w-when can I see them?"

"Ask sir if we can use the projector and I'll show you tomorrow."

"Awesome. It's going to be SO good. I just need to find someone to do the tech and decide when to change the projections. C-could you do it?"

"Billy, are you serious? I'm an artist, not your roadie. Also, technology scares me; I would end up pressing the wrong button and plunging you into darkness. Can't any of The Regulars do it? As well as being the worst jazz musicians the world has ever heard, they're also all massive tech geeks, aren't they?"

"Yeah, I guess. They're all going away for the summer, though, and I'm hoping to line up loads of gigs after this one. I need a techie who is not going anywhere."

"Imagine a life where you went away for the whole summer! Posh tech geeks. Right, so you need someone who's not posh enough to go away all summer and who's daft enough to be persuaded into being your skivvy."

As the words leave her mouth, Blakemore turns the corner and gives us a wave.

"Wassup, losers," he calls with a grin.

After the talent show, Blakemore stopped bullying me. He even started following me around, like he wants to be mates or something. He still calls us losers, but it's in a jokey way now. I wouldn't say that we are friends exactly, but it's way better than when he used to tie me up and punch me in the stomach, that's for sure. And when Mr Osho said I didn't need to give Blakemore maths lessons any more, I thought he looked a bit sad about it.

Now, as he heads towards us, Skyla and I look at each other.

"I think you've found your guy," Skyla says with a wink.

CHAPTER 3

What did the dog say to the insect?

Long time no flea.

Mondays are Mrs Gibbens and Scraggles days. After I tracked him down, Scraggles's new family the Thompsons said they're happy for me to bring him to The Oaks to see Mrs Gibbens regularly. I think having Scraggles back in her life has made Mrs Gibbens very happy. She doesn't have many friends at The Oaks. I think she relied on Granny Bread to cheer her up. She says the visits from me and Scraggles are the highlight of her week.

After school I head over to pick Scraggles up from the Thompsons and walk him over to The Oaks. The carers let me take him into Mrs Gibbens's room, even though dogs are not really allowed. After Granny Bread died – when I couldn't walk up the corridor – we just sat in the reception bit, but then I tried going one step further down the corridor every week. Just like I did when I was scared of standing on the stage before the talent show. Eventually I made it to Mrs Gibbens's door and Scraggles ran straight in and sniffed all of her things. He did a little wee on her handbag, but she just giggled.

Now I'm not scared of the corridor any more, but I still think of Granny Bread every time I walk down it. Last week I remembered the time I visited her after she bought me my drum kit. I was panting so hard after running the whole way. I thought about her face as I ran into the room and gave her a huge hug. It makes me smile remembering that now. I've realized that you can miss someone and still feel happy at the same time.

Whenever I remember something that makes me smile, I give the little bottle of shells that belonged to Granny Bread an extra squeeze before bed and whisper the memory. I know it's a bit weird talking to some shells, but it's like I'm talking to her. Sometimes it's like I can hear her laughing or can hear what she would say back to me. I'm going to take the bottle with me to the gig. I think she would like being in my pocket and coming along.

Me and Mrs Gibbens have a routine now. She watches out of the window for us, always with a face full of make-up and wearing a very strange hat that makes her look a bit like an old lady clown. When she spots us and waves, I let Scraggles off the lead. He belts up the path, waits for the automatic door to open and then dashes into reception and straight up the corridor to her room. He knows exactly where he's going. Today, as I walk up the corridor, I remember doing this same walk, carrying a warm tinfoil package of chocolate brownies, hoping that Granny Bread would like what was inside.

By the time I get there Mrs Gibbens and Scraggles are snuggled on the sofa and Mrs Gibbens is feeding Scraggles squares of cheese. I take my bag off and go to the kitchen to get some squash and put the kettle on. Mrs Gibbens can't walk well any more so I always make us a drink.

"You know Mr and Mrs Thompson n-never feed him t-treats," I say, as she offers Scraggles a sausage. "They say he's got a sensitive t-t-t-tummy."

"Nonsense," she says, and then she lets Scraggles lick her face, which makes me feel quite sick. "You love a cheesy sausage, don't you, my darling?"

"He'll t-t-t-t-turn into a cheesy sausage, the amount you give him."

"He's my baby; he deserves to be spoiled." Then she looks up at me. "As do you, Billy, for bringing my baby to me. Have a look in the cupboard above the kettle."

I know exactly what's going to be in there – a chocolate orange with a pound sellotaped to the top. She gets me one every single week. I once told her I loved them and since then I've had one every Monday, in the same cupboard. At Easter she put a fiver inside the box. I want to tell her that I would come anyway, that she doesn't need to give me presents every week.

"I've told you, Mrs Gibbens, I can't eat all of these chocolate oranges; I've got four at home!"

"Save them for a rainy day or give one to that wonderful little sister of yours. What's her name again?"

"Chloe, and she's not wonderful, she's annoying," I say, offering up a cup of tea and taking a seat on the other side of Scraggles.

Chloe was pestering to meet Scraggles so Mum dropped her off with me one week. Mrs Gibbens kept smiling at her and saying how sweet she was. She's not been back again so I think it might have freaked her out.

I remember how scared I was when I first met Mrs Gibbens. How I'd thought she looked like a skeleton in make-up. Now I know her, she looks completely different to me. Not scary at all.

Last week she let me try all of her hats on. We stood in front of the mirror and posed in different strange hats. I put a yellow one on, with curly antenna-like things poking out of the top, and Mrs Gibbens wore one covered in flowers and then we balanced a purple feathery one on Scraggles's head, picked him up and took a selfie of the three of us. When I showed her the picture, we couldn't stop laughing. Scraggles's tongue was poking out as he tried to lick Mrs Gibbens in the face and my eyes are closed so I look like I'm disgusted by the whole thing. I am going to get it printed out and framed for her birthday.

Mrs Gibbens may be old, but aside from that we're pretty similar. She likes laughing and dogs and being silly just like I do. Loads of the old people in The Oaks remind me of the kids at school. Playing games in the main room and arguing with each other about cheating at cards. That's what the sixth formers do in their common room. It makes me wonder. Do we change that much when we get older, or is it only the outside that changes?

The carers say that Scraggles's visits have "transformed" Mrs Gibbens, given her something to get out of bed for. On my last visit, my favourite carer, Janet, waved at me as I arrived and said, "She can't get herself up and dressed in the morning, but she somehow manages to chop cheese for that dog and get herself to the window to look for him every Monday!"

Back at home later that evening, I'm rereading the email from the pub again to check I haven't missed anything important, when Chloe appears behind me.

"What are you doing?" she whines. Chloe always sounds like she's whining even when she's not.

"Nothing. Leave me alone."

"OK, I won't give you the letter that arrived from Field Fest, then."

Field Fest looks amazing. It's a music festival taking place the weekend before we break up for the summer holidays. I'm going on the Sunday and I can't wait. There are loads of bands playing and there is a comedy tent with some famous comedians too. On the day that I'm there, Leo Leggett is headlining the comedy tent. LEO LEGGETT! He's the biggest comedian ever. He has his own show on telly, *The Leo Leggett Show*, and he sells out massive arenas. I can't wait to see him doing his jokes about Wayne, his dog, miming holding the lead and being pulled along the stage. He's hilarious! Everyone will be shouting his catchphrase at him: "GET IN THE TOILET!" People wear T-shirts with his face on the front and the catchphrase on the back. He is exactly who I want to be. Maybe this summer will be my first step in becoming like Leo. Maybe it will be *my* face on everyone's T-shirt one day.

I begged Mum and Dad to let me go to Field Fest. They made me do tons of chores until I had earned enough money to get three tickets. I'm taking Skyla and I wanted one of The Regulars to come, but they're all busy with cricket matches or weddings so I have a spare ticket. Dad got himself a ticket too. He's coming with us, but he's promised to just leave us to it. He's excited about some terrible old-man band playing on the other side of the site from the comedy tent so we should get rid of him pretty quickly.

Now I turn round in my chair and see that Chloe's holding a big envelope with the Field Fest logo printed on it. As I go to grab it, she screams and runs out of the kitchen, still squealing as I tear after her.

"Give it to me!" I call.

"Only if you let me come to Field Fest."

Ever since she heard I had a spare ticket Chloe has been pestering me to come. She is also OBSESSED with Leo Leggett. I don't want her there, though. I don't need my little sister hanging around me all day, and Mum and Dad say she's too young anyway.

"OK." I smile. "You can come."

"Really?" she gasps, relaxing her grip on the envelope.

"Yeah," I say, snatching it from her. "If you s-save some money and buy yourself a t-t-ticket!"

"Billy!" she screams.

Mum waddles in, red in the face.

"Will you two stop shouting, for goodness' sake?"

I dash up to my room and open the envelope. It has a shiny brochure listing all of the performers. There are also four Field Fest tickets, a pen and a map of the site. I trace my finger over the picture of the comedy tent, imagining the stage. It looks huge!

I picture Leo Leggett looking at the same map. Looking forward to wowing yet another adoring crowd. By the time I get to Field Fest I will have done my first gig. I will be a proper comedian by then, just like him.

CHAPTER 4

What kind of underwear do maths teachers wear?

Algebras.

Skyla's not in school for the rest of the week. Every time I look at her empty desk I picture her head collapsing on to it. I hope she's OK. I don't know what to do. She won't answer my texts and calls. I feel helpless.

Today in the Music Lounge, me and Mr Osho are playing *Forbidden Island* while Alex, Josh and Matthew all try and get their maths homework finished before next period. I don't know why they always leave it so late. Watching kids do their homework on the bus or resting it on their arm as they literally walk into the lesson stresses me out. I always do it the day it's set. Other kids call me a geek and a try-hard, but I don't see how waiting until the last minute makes them any cooler than me. I'm the one chilling out listening to tunes and playing board games and they are the ones sweating over geometry.

We still come to the Music Lounge most lunchtimes. The drums got taken back to the rehearsal rooms after the talent show so the band haven't been practising much the last couple of months. I won't have time for band stuff anyway, and the others are going away for the summer. Maybe The Regulars can do a comeback gig for our fans when we're in Year Eight.

Just as we are about to collect the final piece of treasure, Mr Osho says quietly, "You and Skyla are tight, aren't you, Billy?"

"Yes, sir."

"She's been off school a lot recently. Do you know if anything is going on at home?"

"I don't know, sir. Has her mum not called in sick for her?"

"She did, yes. We spoke briefly on the phone. I thought you may know a bit more from Skyla."

"She won't talk about it," I say, wondering if I should tell Mr Osho how worried I am about her. Then I think about what Skyla would do if she knew I was talking to a teacher about her, and I feel instantly guilty.

"She's pretty tough."

Mr Osho nods his head slowly.

"Well, if she talks to you and there's a problem, you know that I'm here, don't you?"

"Of course, sir."

We take our pieces and leave the island before it sinks.

"We are g-g-getting too good at this, sir."

"The dream team. I'm going to change the record. It looks like the boys need a little help over there."

I look over and Matthew has his head in his hands. Alex and Josh don't look much more enthusiastic.

"All right, b-b-boys," I call. "Do you n-need a geometry teacher?"

They nod and beckon me over.

"I used to know one," I say, smiling. "But they can't help. They sprained their angle. Get it?!"

They groan. My jokes get more groans than laughs from The Regulars now. I think I need to work on my material. The only person who still really laughs at my jokes is Chloe, but she's nine and laughs at Dad when he pretends to walk down fake stairs, so I don't feel that encouraged by it, if I'm honest.

"Can we copy yours, Billy?" Alex asks, as I sit down.

"No one is copying anyone," comes Mr Osho's voice. It's easy to forget that he's a teacher sometimes.

Once in form class I was pretending to pull one of my teeth out to make Josh laugh and Mr Osho told me off in front of the whole class. I went bright red. It was a weird feeling, being told off by a teacher that I like. It was embarrassing.

"Billy can help you if he wants, but he is not getting his book out for you to look at, OK?"

As I'm trying to explain a question on angles to them, Blakemore swings the door open. I don't know why he crashes into rooms instead of just walking in like a normal person, but you always know about it when Blakemore arrives.

"All right, losers, what you doing?" Then he sees the maths books. "Oh, brilliant, are we copying Billy's homework?"

Mr Osho looks up again. "No, we are not, William."

"Sorry, sir."

Blakemore sits next to me but doesn't even bother getting his maths book out. He's in the bottom set anyway so he wouldn't have the same homework. When the others finally get it and start scratching away with their pencils, Blakemore looks at me.

"What you doing for the summer, Plimpton?"

I remember what Skyla said about him being my techie and think about the gig. It's only a week away. I really need to sort out who will play the projections. Me and Blakemore are OK now. He's still a bit mean to some kids. I saw him throwing Elliot's lunch bag over the playground wall last week, but he never does it when he's near me. I think he knows that I would tell on him. Or that it would remind me of when he was like that to me. Mr Osho said that helping him was the best thing I could have done, for both of us. Now we kind of understand each other better.

"Well," I say, "my mum's having a baby at the end of August so we aren't going anywhere. Also, I'm going to do some comedy gigs."

"What, real ones with grown-ups watching?"

"Yeah. I've already got a slot at the King's Head next weekend."

"No way?! That's awesome."

I look at his face and wonder if I should ask. I

still don't fully trust Blakemore, but I need to train someone up on the tech. I can't think of anyone else apart from Chloe or Dad. Chloe would probably end up accidentally playing some horse film instead of the projections and the idea of my dad doing it is just too embarrassing. I couldn't look more like a little kid who doesn't belong in a comedy club than if I have my dad tagging along next to me all the time. I have told him to pretend he's not with me at the pub. So I look at Blakemore and ask the question.

"W-W-W-What are you doing next Friday night?" I say. The Regulars all look at me. Their faces screwing up into a thousand questions.

"Nothing. Why?"

Before I can change my mind I blurt it out: "I need a techie for the show if you're interested."

Alex looks up from his book and frowns at me. He still can't believe that I'm nice to Blakemore after how horrible he used to be to us.

Alex goes quiet whenever Blakemore tries to hang around with us. I don't think he will ever trust him. When I told him about Blakemore forcing me to write my name on the talent show list and how that all led up to me playing with The Regulars and then ditching them for Teenplay, he was furious. He said we wouldn't have fallen out if it wasn't for Blakemore. I agree, but without him interfering, I would also probably have never made it on to that stage. Not that I'm grateful to Blakemore, but maybe that's why I can forgive him.

Looking at Alex's face makes me feel silly, like maybe I'm wrong to ask him. Or like I should be tougher. So I give it a try.

"You'll have to do exactly what I say. You would be my staff, so I can tell you what to do." I try to sound confident, like a celebrity giving orders.

It obviously doesn't sound quite right as Josh and Alex start giggling and mimicking me: *"You'll have to do what I say."*

Blakemore scowls, but he's thinking about it, I can tell.

"What's in it for me?" he asks. I know I've already got him, though. Blakemore hates it at home. He would do anything to get away from his older brother. I remember seeing them at football, his brother grabbing and shoving him.

"I've got a spare ticket to Field Fest the weekend after. You can have that."

He doesn't even pretend to think about it. "Yeah, all right then."

"When I get the images from Skyla, we will need to rehearse so you know what you're doing, OK?" Blakemore nods and grins. He's chuffed, I can tell.

"I wish I wasn't going to a stupid wedding," Josh moans. "I want to go to Field Fest."

Mr Osho comes and joins us.

"Ooh, are you going to Field Fest, Billy? Promise me you'll go to the jazz stage. The line-up is incredible. I might even see you there."

"Are you going, sir?"

"Yeah, I go every year. What's this I'm hearing about a stand-up gig as well? Are you performing at the festival?"

"I w-w-wish, sir! No, I've got a slot at the comedy night at the King's Head next Friday!"

"That's amazing, Billy! I'll definitely come – if you don't mind having your embarrassing teacher in the audience."

"You're not embarrassing, sir. It's th-this lot that are embarrassing."

Josh jumps up and sits on me. "Embarrassing, are we, Plimpton?!" Then the others pile on too and I am squashed underneath them until I tell them that they are not remotely embarrassing.

As the bell goes, I smile. I can't believe I have such good mates and I've got my first real shot at stardom in exactly one week! I never thought that this would be my life. I don't even feel nervous; this is the right thing for me to be doing. I'm on the right path, I can feel it.

CHAPTER 5

Did you hear about the artist who always took things too far?

She didn't know where to draw the line.

I practise my set in the mirror all weekend until I'm bored of hearing my own voice. Sometimes I get through the whole thing without stammering once. I bet I stammer loads at the gig, though; it's different when it's just me and the mirror. But it's OK if I do, I have stuff I can say about it onstage, and since the talent show I'm not so scared of stammering in front of people. As long as I'm in control and can address it with the audience how I want to, then it feels fine. It might even add to the show – make it interesting for people. It's good for people to hear a stammer onstage, then they won't be so shocked if they hear one in a shop or on the bus. I think we should have people who stammer reading the news and on the radio.

At school on Monday it already feels like the end of term, even though we still have two and a half weeks to go. All the teachers are trying to wind things down. They clear their desks and take things off the wall. Some of them do lessons outside, which means we mess about, squirting water bottles at each other in the sun for an hour; the sensible teachers stick us in front of a film.

In history with Shouty Man we watch a boring documentary about the Tudors, but in some lessons, they don't even try and make us watch something related to the subject. In food tech we watch *Finding Dory*. Everyone groans and tells Mrs Peat that we are too old, but she just presses play and carries on messing with the fruit and vegetable displays.

She's been super strict with us ever since Blakemore took one of the chillies and microwaved it until it exploded. We all had to be evacuated. When Mrs Peat opened the microwave door it created a toxic gas. Everyone was coughing and putting their jumpers over their faces and then bumping into each other because they couldn't see. It was really funny, but Mrs Peat got so cross. She kept shouting, "Cover your eyes!" in this high-pitched voice that we had never heard her use before. In the "Reason for Detention" section on Blakemore's detention slip she wrote:

For theft and dangerous misuse of school property.

When he showed me, Blakemore was really annoyed. "I didn't steal it. She makes it sound way worse than it was. All I did was microwave a chilli in food tech. A chilli is food and a microwave is tech. I was doing the right thing for once! How was I meant to know it would make everyone cry?"

"I guess she couldn't write 'microwaving a chilli', though, could she?"

"Why?" He shrugged. "That's what I did. I didn't thieve it. She could have put it back on the display after. I can't win."

He has a point. It's like Blakemore can't help but get into trouble. The more negatives he gets, the less likely he is to behave.

I'm not sure the whole giving-out-negatives thing works for some kids. If I got ten negatives every day, and everyone told me I was bad, I think I would give up and believe I was bad too. Mr Osho never gives out negatives. He keeps people behind after class and tries to come up with ways to help. Like the time I taught Blakemore maths – that was way better than giving out detentions, even though neither of us thought it at the time.

Skyla ignored my calls and messages all weekend. But today she comes in at lunchtime. She looks tired, but I'm so relieved to see her that I don't mention the bags under her eyes. When she finds me in the dinner hall she steals a handful of chips off my tray and says, "Mr Osho said we can use his projector. Do you want to see my works of art?"

"Yeah!" I say, offering up the last of my chips. "Let's find Blakemore."

"You did not actually ask him?!"

"It was your idea!"

"OK, we'll get him on the way. Who'd have thought Billy and Blakemore – taking the comedy world by storm."

As we head out of the hall, I decide she seems pretty relaxed and risk a question. "How come you weren't in this morning?" I say, as breezily as I can.

"Mum stuff," she says.

She doesn't seem too annoyed, so I risk another: "What's wrong with her?"

"She's having one of her rough patches, but she'll be fine."

Then, just as I think I might actually be able to find out what's going on, I feel a hand on my shoulder.

"All right, losers?"

"Just the man – you've rescued me from being interrogated by Billy here," Skyla says, pulling me and Blakemore into a loose headlock. "Let's get this show on the road, boys."

We head to form class. Mr Osho is on his phone but waves us in and points to the projector. I hope the pub will have a projector I can use on the night. I've emailed them, but they haven't answered yet. I want the cartoons to become my "thing". Something that people talk about more than my stammer. I want to be described as the hilarious kid with the projections, not the kid with the stammer. People feeling sorry for you really gets in the way of making them laugh.

When I did the news interview after the talent show I didn't stammer once. I think the interviewers were disappointed. They kept saying things like, "Well, today you seem to be speaking very confidently." As if it was a bad thing, or like I was a fraud. Actually, after the talent show, my stammer totally disappeared for a bit. I got worried that it might have gone for ever and then I wouldn't be able to do my jokes about it any more. But I needn't have worried; it came back stronger than ever in January and it's not gone anywhere since, though it doesn't ruin my life like it used to. It did make me think, though – can I tell jokes about having a stammer if I don't have one? I'm not sure. The important thing is that I need to be funny with or without it.

Some days I don't stammer much – well, I do but not so much that anyone else would notice. I have found little tricks around some stammers. Making words a bit more sing-song or stretching the start out a bit. Kind of different versions of the stuff that Sue, my old speech therapist, taught me.

Some days it comes back with a vengeance. Like the day when Mr Johnson made me read out my history essay in front of everyone. I stammered so badly on the word "battle" that every muscle in my face tensed up. My throat got so tight I thought I was either going to be sick or get stuck like that for ever. None of my tricks worked that day. But most days it's way easier. Most kids at school seem to have got used to just waiting for me to finish and if they don't it doesn't bother me as much when they interrupt me or finish my sentences.

Mum always says it takes a bit of practice to learn how to wait. She says that sometimes even she finds it hard to wait for me to finish speaking – especially when she's busy and I'm trying to tell her something or we are all sitting round the table together. If *she* sometimes finds it hard, then it's no wonder it's difficult for everyone else.

I've also been working on my comebacks. A comeback is what you say to someone in the audience who shouts out. Shouting out is called heckling; it happens all the time in real comedy clubs. Apparently, every comedian needs a good comeback. Some people have really cruel ones that embarrass the person in the audience, which makes them shut up.

But I don't want to be cruel. I know what it's like to have people poke fun at me, and I don't want to do it to anyone else. I've decided that my comeback is going to be, "You can't heckle me, I'm a kid – I'll tell my mum on you. She's old and she's hormonal." I think that's quite funny. I thought I could even get my phone out and pretend to ring her and cry down the phone. I've practised in the mirror.

"Mummy, there's a mean man on the second row and he says I'm not funny." Then I do a massive fake cry.

Anyway, thinking about hecklers and comebacks is making me nervous so I'll stop. It's going to be great, isn't it? It has to be. It's what I've been waiting for all year.

When Skyla is all set up, we click on the file and the first image comes up on to the whiteboard. I can't help but gasp. The drawing is so cool. It's a massive cartoon version of me wrapped up in a huge snake. I stand in front of the screen with the picture behind me. I imagine the stage and the audience and then begin.

"I got a pet snake for C-C-Christmas, but my mum is completely terrified of it." Then I start doing an impression of my mum squealing and standing on a table. Mr Osho puts his phone down and comes over to watch the show.

"I don't know what her problem is, the snake's completely 'armless!"

Mr Osho and Skyla laugh, but Blakemore frowns.

"I don't get it."

Skyla giggles at him and whispers, "Harmless – arm less," gesturing to her arms.

He nods slowly.

Skyla changes the image to one of me sitting in an exam surrounded by papers and drawings.

I smile. "I failed my art exam the other day," I say. I decide I'll try and milk the moment a bit more. "I failed my art exam the other day." I pull a sad face and put my hand to my ear, clearly waiting for some sympathy until Skyla and Mr Osho get it.

"Ahhhh."

Blakemore still looks gormless. I keep going to the punchline.

"I think I used th-the wrong pencil. N-N-Never mind, maybe it just wasn't … 2B."

When Blakemore still looks confused, I give up.

"T-Tough crowd!" I say, as I sit up on one of the desks. "Let's j-just look at the projections, Skyla. I'll explain the j-j-jokes to you another d-day, Blakemore."

As she flicks through the drawings, I can picture them up on the wall behind the stage. They're perfect. I think it will make me stand out from the other comedians. Not that I need much help standing out as a twelve-year-old with a stammer. I'm not sure there are many other comics out there quite like me.

Skyla's done pictures for all of my top ten jokes. I found some in a new joke book I got from the school library, but I changed them so they sound a bit less like jokes and more like stories from my life. I've realized I can make stuff up. It doesn't all have to be true, like the snake thing: I obviously didn't get a snake for Christmas, but the audience won't know that. If people think you're talking to them about real stuff, the joke surprises them and they laugh even more. I hope they laugh on Friday!

I think about how Blakemore didn't laugh. Maybe I need to get some more live practice in. Tonight is my weekly visit to Mrs Gibbens. Maybe I can do a show for her, although Mrs Gibbens is usually too busy kissing Scraggles to laugh at my jokes.

It's still worth a try. I want this show to be perfect!

CHAPTER 6

Comic Sans, Times New Roman and Arial walk into a bar.

The bartender yells, "Get out, we don't serve your type."

It's the day of the gig. Blakemore and Skyla come over after school to rehearse the technical stuff. Blakemore turns out to be pretty good with computers and he knows how to sort the projections out. He's not so good at following the script, but he's fine when he's watching me and following cues that way.

Dad walks us down to the pub and stands at the bar with a pint. Next to him sits an old man who's quietly talking to himself. When we introduce ourselves to the barman, he calls over the bar and a lady with a shiny blondish mullet and a ring on every finger shows us the stage upstairs. The room smells musty and the floor is sticky.

We go out on to the little stage, looking for a surface to project the animations on to, but there isn't one.

The mullet lady mutters, "It's like a sodding school play."

I'm not sure if she wants us to hear or not and so I pretend I haven't. I start to feel the nerves flood through my body. My brain feels busy and my skin tingles, but I ignore it. I look out towards where the audience will be sitting and try to imagine the smiling faces and the laughter.

It feels very different to the talent show and TV interview. The chairs are still stacked up and there are empty crisp packets on the floor. And I won't be able to use Skyla's amazing cartoons.

"It's OK, I-I w-w-will do it without them," I say, trying to smile. "We can save them for the next gig."

We head back down to the bar where the football is playing loudly on a load of huge screens around the pub. The room is busier now, but no one looks like they are here for a comedy night. None of the faces staring up at the football even look like they could smile, let alone laugh. Big men with bald heads and thick necks. I imagine their angry faces staring back at me as I get stuck on a punchline. I'm starting to panic inside. Maybe this was a terrible idea.

I have to practise in front of real people, though, don't I? It's the reality of being a stand-up comedian. On the comedy forum I read it says that the "comedy circuit" is made up of hundreds of pubs and little comedy clubs and rooms all over the country, and that it's the circuit that allows comedians to earn a living. I have to do this if I want to be a proper comedian and not just some kid who did a school talent show once.

Dad buys us a Coke each and when it's fifteen minutes to showtime we all go upstairs. The lady with the rings is huffing as she puts the chairs out and so we go and help.

"I-Is there anywhere that I c-c-can wait backstage?" I ask. I don't want to be standing around when the audience arrive.

"Backstage?! La-di-da! Where do you think you are?" She laughs to herself and I go red. Then she says, "You can wait in the bog at the back. Hide in a cubicle and come out when you hear your name."

I look at Skyla, Dad and Blakemore, who all look as terrified as I feel.

"You don't have to do this, Billy," Dad says gently.

"Yeah, I d-d-do." They go to sit down at the back of the empty room. On my way to the toilet I see Alex and Matthew arrive and look around the room. I asked them to sit at the back so I wouldn't get distracted. I want it to feel like it will when I'm on the comedy circuit for real, when I don't have people I know there.

I go into the toilet. As I sit on the grotty toilet lid I can feel my heart starting to race. I try to breathe calmly in and out, but the stench of the wee makes me not want to breathe at all. I reach into my pocket for Granny Bread's shells, but it's empty and I realize that I have left them at home.

I can't do a gig without Granny Bread! I stand up and try to pace around the tiny cubicle, like a stressed battery chicken, wondering if there is any way out of this. If I should make a run for it.

Just as I'm hesitating, I hear the lady with the mullet start talking into the microphone. I close my eyes and even though I don't have the shells, I try to imagine what Granny Bread would say. *"Go for it, Billy. I'm so proud I could pop."*

The lady doesn't sound any more enthusiastic now that she's on the stage than she did earlier.

"We're trying this comedy thing out. Hopefully it will get better. This month Roger has booked a kid who is currently hiding in the back bog, so it's probably good there aren't many of you."

I'm wondering exactly how many is "not many" when she calls my name. I unlock the door, breathe in my last lungful of wee-filled air and step out.

The room looks almost exactly the same as when I left it. Dad and my friends are at the back and in front of them there are rows and rows of empty chairs. On the second row from the front sits a couple who are wearing matching waterproof jackets and on the other side is a group of four blokes in white T-shirts and caps. Mr Osho is in the middle, grinning from ear to ear. In the front row is a girl who must be in her twenties; she's holding a pen and notebook. I want to turn round and go straight back into the toilet.

I slowly walk up to the stage, wishing that something would save me. That something will happen to rescue me. Nothing does and I find myself standing on the stage, taking the microphone from its stand.

"Shall I just g-g-g-go and lock myself b-b-b-b-back in the t-toilet?"

Dad and Blakemore look really worried and Skyla has her head in her hands. Mr Osho chuckles. The couple smile when I say this, and the girl writes on her pad. I see the blokes lean into each other and start talking.

"Yeah," I say to them. "I am a k-k-k-kid and, yeah, I c-c-c-can't speak properly either." The microphone makes a horrible squeaky sound, "And apparently I can't work a microphone either."

The matching couple smile but the four men keep talking. Then they pick up their pints and stand up.

"Soz, little fella, we thought they were showing the football on a big screen up here." They walk out of the room, still talking loudly.

I try desperately to think of a comeback. None of the ones I've practised make any sense in this situation, but I can't ignore the fact that they have walked out, can I? I end up feebly shouting, "Bye! I hope your team loses!" Which sounds sad and bitter and way less funny out loud than it sounded in my head.

I've barely started and I've already lost half of my audience. My mouth has gone dry and my head feels like it's going to explode. I look at the couple in their matching jackets and the girl on the front row and take a deep breath. I try to listen to my thoughts. I walk away from the microphone and sit on the front of the stage.

"I really d-don't need a m-microphone to talk to three people, do I? No offence to the rest of you," I say to the others, "but you're my friends, my dad and my teacher – you don't count as people."

Mr Osho laughs loudly at this and the sound seems to echo around the empty room. Dad waves back at me, smiling. I'm surprised by how smoothly I'm talking. My mouth is still completely dry and I'm sweating, but for some reason my stammer is not joining in with the rest of my body today.

"Yeah, I don't need to amplify the next ten minutes. I would actually p-prefer to whisper it. Then we might all be able to forget it quicker." The girl at the front is scribbling and so I just focus on the matching puffa couple who are really smiling. "I w-w-would walk out too, but I need to practise. You see, I want to be a famous stand-up c-comedian."

The couple say, "Ooooh!" and I say, "I know. So, if you can j-j-just stay there for t-t-ten minutes, I will tell some jokes, you'll smile and nod and then we can all go home and pretend this n-never happened, OK?"

I then tell them all my favourite jokes. Even without the microphone my voice sounds loud and the time seems to go on for ever. My lips keep sticking to my teeth. Then my stammer decides to show up to the party after all. It totally stops me from getting to the end of a joke about a shellfish. My mouth becomes so dry I can't swallow.

This is not how the gig was supposed to go. There was meant to be laughter. I was meant to enjoy it, not feel like it was the biggest mistake of my life. Maybe I'm not meant to be a comedian after all. Maybe the talent show was a fluke. Maybe it was the high point of my life and now everything will get worse. My joke book jokes don't even sound funny to me any more. I sound like a stupid little kid telling bad dad jokes. Then I realize, that's exactly what I am. I'm not a comedian. I didn't even make these jokes up.

I shouldn't be here.

The thoughts are getting louder and louder in my head as my mouth somehow manages to start the final joke.

"My auntie's pet tortoise fell into her toilet the other day."

The woman on the front is scribbling things on to her pad. I almost haven't got the energy to say the punchline.

"It must have thought it was a turdle."

The couple smile and nod like I asked. I say thank you and walk back to the toilet and lock myself inside.

CHAPTER 7

Why did Tigger look in the toilet?

He was looking for Pooh.

Mum is waiting in the kitchen when we get home. I stomp straight upstairs and she calls after me. I go into my room and sit on the bed, knowing that she will follow. She comes in and sits next to me and I try and cuddle into her without squashing the bump.

"You don't have to talk about it, Billy, if you don't want to. But know that things are never as bad as you think."

That's when the tears come. "It w-w-was w-w-w-w-worse th-than b-b-b-b-bad," I sob. Between the sobbing and the stammering, it's almost impossible to get a single word out. Mum just holds me until I calm down enough to whisper. "It was terrible, Mum. It was the worst n-n-night of my life."

She smiles at me and strokes my cheek.

"Was it worse than the time your trousers fell down at that fancy restaurant?" I can't help smiling at the memory. She'd told me the trousers were too big, but I hadn't listened. I'd thought I looked cool.

"Yes! Way worse," I say, trying to hold on to my sadness.

"And worse than the time you walked into the patio doors at Auntie Sausage's wedding?"

I smile and nod and then whisper, "Standing on that stage in that p-p-pub made me wish the floor w-would literally open up and swallow me whole. My mouth was so dry it felt like I had a cardboard tongue. I can't even explain how bad it was, Mum. I can't do it. I can't be a comedian. It's too hard."

I weep into her jumper and she cuddles me until I eventually fall asleep.

When I wake in the morning, things are no better. The pub has sent an email telling me that the woman on the front row was a reviewer for *The Herald*. So that's why she was jotting things down! I don't want to see what she has said, but at the same time I really do. I can't stop myself even though I know it will be really bad. Like when you know if you eat the rest of the sweets you will want to vomit, but you eat them anyway. I bring up the review on my phone, grab my Granny Bread shells, squeeze them tight and say, "You weren't with me for the gig, Granny Bread, but you are here for the review."

I imagine her voice: *"Don't listen to anything they say, Billy. You are wonderful exactly as you are."*

I smile and look down at the screen.

A grotty pub room with a non-existent audience would be a tough gig for a seasoned professional, and it proved to be too much for twelve-year-old Billy Plimpton. One has to wonder what price the children of today are paying when they take to our stages and screens in search of fame. The gig was at points difficult to watch and some of the audience left during the young stand-up's short set. It was not all tragic, however – in between some terrible jokes clearly taken from Christmas crackers, a nervous Plimpton managed to charm the remaining tiny audience with his witty conversational style. If the harrowing experience has not put the young comic off for life, then he could have a future ahead. If I had to put money on it, however, I doubt we will be seeing Plimpton on a stage any time soon. There are not many people who would come back from such a tough gig.

Review by Rowena Belige
⭐ ⭐ *TWO STARS.*

After I have read the words about ten times, I turn it off and look at my shells. "She's right, Granny Bread. Everything she said is right. My jokes *are* terrible. It *was* a horrible gig and she *definitely* won't be seeing me on a stage again. She only gave me two stars because I'm a kid and giving me one would have seemed too mean." I sigh. I can't even imagine what Granny Bread would say to comfort me.

When I go downstairs, Dad looks up from his phone and I can tell that he has seen the review. Mum has made my favourite pancakes so I know that she's read it too.

After a hideous silence, Dad says, "It's not all bad, Billy. She said some nice things too."

"Are you serious?" I say, a bit louder than I mean to. "She basically told the world that I died on my arse!"

"Watch your language, Billy Plimpton," Mum snaps.

"That's what it's called, Mum, when a gig goes really badly. Dying on your—"

"Bottom. Thank you," Mum interrupts.

"OK, OK, well, I totally died on my … bum, and now everyone in the whole world knows it! My career is over. I might as well have farted in front of the King."

Then Chloe walks in. "Who's farted in front of the King?"

"NO ONE!" Mum and Dad say in unison.

I'm doing extra Scraggles walks this weekend for the Thompsons and so I head to Mrs Gibbens and read the review to her while she feeds Scraggles some Quavers. She's so focused on the dog I'm not sure if she's listening, but when I get to the end, for some reason she grins and claps her hands.

"This is meant to be the tough bit, Billy! That's why you've got to keep going."

"I think I might give up on comedy, Mrs Gibbens," I say. I sit back and start eating Quavers with Scraggles, feeling more sorry for myself than I have for a very long time. More sorry than the time Blakemore made me stammer my way through the alphabet in the toilets, more sorry than when I broke Mum's great-grandma's vase playing football in the living room, even more sorry than when I ditched The Regulars to drum for Teenplay. I sigh a big sigh and Scraggles sighs too, as though he knows how I feel.

At least I have Field Fest to look forward to. I can be a normal kid for the day and let the proper comedians do all the work.

As I'm walking Scraggles back home in the drizzle, he stops and sniffs and I know he is about to poo. Which is all I need.

Picking up Scraggles's poo is totally disgusting. I'm pretty sure Mrs Gibbens would not feed him quite so many cheesy sausages if she had to do it. Still, I have got the perfect technique now. At first, I didn't know what I was doing and the bag blew around in the wind and I ended up with poo on my finger, but now I am a poo-picking master. I even wrote a list.

THE DOS AND DON'TS OF POO-PICKING

- DO NOT use the thin and flimsy bags. If your finger goes through a bag and makes contact you will never forget that feeling. EVER.

- DO place your hand right inside the bag, making sure the hand and wrist are covered. This minimizes risk of contact.
- DO NOT leave a poo bag dangling on a tree, thinking you will collect it on the way back. You will definitely forget and create the illusion that your town is filled with disgusting poo fairies.
- DO stand into the wind. The edges of the bag will be blown in the right direction. However, the smell will also be blown towards you so…
- DO NOT breathe in through your nose (or through your mouth – if you do this then you can taste it. Ideally just hold your breath).
- DO smile sweetly at any dog owner who doesn't pick up after their dog and say something like, "What a shame! You must have forgotten your bags. Here, let me lend you one. I'm sure you wouldn't want to leave it there for an innocent kid like me to tread in, would you?"
- DO NOT ever assume that one poo bag is enough when setting off for a walk.

(Scraggles once needed five. I ran out of bags and had to use a leaf and a stick and balance my way to the bin like I was taking part in some kind of horrific egg and spoon race.)

- DO try to enjoy the feeling of warmth through the bag. (At first it made me retch, but now I don't mind it so much – especially on a cold day. It's like a disgusting hand-warmer.)

- DO NOT ever, under any circumstances, attempt to break the record for how many times you can swing the filled bag around your finger – however tempting. Yes, the bag may be sealed, but believe me they split open more easily than you think. I once arrived at Mrs Gibbens's with poo on my jeans – I broke the record for number of spins, but it definitely wasn't worth it.

- The DOs and DO NOTs of runny ones – I still have absolutely no idea, any thoughts or advice would be most welcome.

Despite knowing the dos and don'ts of poo-picking, it's still a pretty horrid thing to have to do. Today

Scraggles poos in the middle of the road and I have to stop traffic to pick it up. Two men in a white van are laughing at me and beep their horn as they eventually drive past.

There is no poo bin for the rest of the way, so I am stuck in the drizzle, carrying poo. Sometimes the universe just makes everything worse.

I wonder what I will do with my life now that I won't be a stand-up comedian. As I gently swing the poo bag I remember the dry mouth and empty seats. The silences after the punchlines. I shudder. *Never again*, I think. Never again.

My comedy dreams are over.

CHAPTER 8

**Why couldn't Black Beauty's foal make a
speech at the festival?**

She was a little horse.

The week passes uneventfully, until finally, the
weekend is here and we're on our way to Field Fest.
As we drive over the hill and the site comes into view,
my face freezes. The festival is HUGE. There is a sea
of people shoaling like fish into the main entrance
and behind them are the enormous marquees and
stages that I have only ever seen on TV. I squeeze
Granny Bread's bottle of shells tightly in my pocket.
I look at all the smiling people and the flags waving
in the breeze. She would love it here.

I imagine what she would say: "*Eh, Billy, who'd*

have thought I would become a festival chick? Isn't it magical how life turns out?"

We park and clamber out. Through the entrance I can see glimpses of people wearing costumes and sequins and swirling fire sticks and huge flags on tall poles.

"Th-Th-This is a b-b-bit bigger than I thought!"

"It's massive!" says Blakemore. I've never seen Blakemore so jolly. When he knocked on the door this morning – half an hour early – with a huge grin on his face, I realized something. I've never seen Blakemore at a birthday party or even at the park. Maybe he doesn't get asked to join in with many things. I'm glad I invited him, even though Chloe will never forgive me for not bringing her. Skyla doesn't seem to mind him being here either. I think she finds him quite funny.

We've made a plan of who we are going to watch. First up, some new comedians in the family tent, then Blakemore is dragging us to see this metal band that he likes, and Skyla wants to see some singer-songwriter called Josh Something at five o'clock. All singer-songwriters seem to be called Josh Something, and they all have floppy hair and beads round their neck. Then we're heading over to see Leo Leggett; we all agreed on that one.

71

When we get to the entrance, I see a sign saying: ARTISTS. I realize that now I'll never get to go through that door. Just looking at it makes me feel sad.

We head in through the main entrance and towards a yellow tent. A woman with locs scans our tickets and then puts pink wristbands on us. She fastens mine too tightly and it pinches my little arm hairs, but I'm too excited to complain. Skyla asks which way the family tent is and the woman tells us where to go, but she's talking quickly and I'm too distracted to pay attention.

"Follow the blue and white flags all the way down past the vegan food stalls, left through the Magical Meadow and then, when you get to the sign for the children's field, the family tent is the yellow and purple marquee on your right."

As we walk into the festival, the thrum of music hits us. I can feel it in my body, vibrating through the floor. I stop to take it all in. The smell of frying onions and the stalls of glow-up necklaces.

Dad puts his arm round my shoulders and says, "Now, I know you want to get rid of me as soon as possible, but shall I take you to the family tent first?"

"Yes, please," I say, sounding like a little kid.

When we get to the tent, I'm feeling slightly less overwhelmed by the size of the place. I've looked at the map and have got my bearings. The whole festival revolves around the main stage with all the other tents and stages surrounding it. You can tell where you are by which bit of the main stage you're looking at. Dad still doesn't seem too happy leaving us, but when I point out where everything is, that seems to reassure him.

"OK, we're going to meet back here after Leo Leggett at eight o'clock. Yes?"

"Can we stay a bit later, though, if we're having fun?" I ask.

"Festivals at night can get a bit dodgy, Billy. I think you'll have seen enough by then. Now, are you sure you don't want me to stay with you?"

"Yeah, I'm sure."

"Well, call me if you change your mind and text me every hour like we agreed, so I know you're OK."

"I'll look after him," Skyla says, leaning her elbow on my shoulder, as if she's years older than me.

There is no one onstage in the tent when we walk inside, but there are families sitting on the floor and some kids running around doing cartwheels. I hope no one is going to be doing cartwheels when the comedian is on. That would be distracting for them.

Now that I truly understand how hard it is, I almost feel nervous for whoever is about to walk out on to the stage.

We sit down near the front and wait. The programme said there should be a comedian on right now, someone I've never heard of. Everyone is chatting and shuffling about, and then a lady with a clipboard and a walkie-talkie walks on to the stage and everyone shushes.

"Welcome to the family tent, everyone!" she says. She's clearly nervous – she can't be the comedian. What kind of comedian carries a walkie-talkie?

"I have some bad news, I'm afraid. The comedian we booked is unwell and won't make it to open the show today. Luckily, we have bumped our wonderful circus performer up the bill, and they should be here any minute. After that there will be a gap while we wait for our next act – so if any of you would like a chance to perform your first festival gig come and find me backstage!" She laughs, clearly not expecting anyone to take her up on the offer.

Skyla nudges me. I shake my head.

"I c-c-can't," I whisper, remembering the horror of

the pub. Just then, though, Blakemore grabs my hand and forces it into the air.

"He'll do it, miss!" he shouts up at the lady. Then he adds, "He's a proper comedian. You might have seen him on telly!"

My face goes instantly red and hot and I pull my arm back down and shake my head.

"N-N-No, B-Blakemore, stop it!"

The woman is beaming at me. "Well, it looks like we have a volunteer! Come and see me backstage and we can set you up! Enjoy the show, everyone." She walks off the stage.

"What the hell are you doing?" I hiss at Blakemore. I stand up and storm out of the tent and walk straight into Mr Osho.

"Hey, Billy! What's going on, buddy? You don't look like you've got good festival vibes." Skyla and Blakemore come straight out of the tent after me. I don't say anything so Mr Osho looks at them.

"I thought it would be perfect, sir," Blakemore says, looking confused.

"They offered him a gig, sir, in there," Skyla says, pointing back at the tent. "You did say you wanted more gigs, Billy. What happened to your summer of comedy?"

"That w-was before last week," I whisper. "The gig in the pub was so awful, I don't think I ever want to go on a stage again."

"It wasn't THAT bad," Skyla says. "There just weren't enough people. There are way more here now, look."

I look round at the tent. She's right, there are more people. The little girl is still doing cartwheels. I think about my comeback in case I get heckled. I can't tell a little kid doing cartwheels that I'm going to tell my mum on them, can I?

"It'll be loads better," Skyla goes on. "You can't give up because of one tough gig, Billy. Can he, sir?"

I look at Mr Osho. He always knows what to say.

"I thought last week's gig was great," he says. "It was tough, but you were brilliant and brave. But Skyla, only Billy can decide if this is the right time to get back on the stage—"

"Wait!" Skyla snaps her fingers, her eyes wide with excitement. "I've got an idea." She turns to Blakemore. "Have you got the projections saved on your phone?" He nods. "We could use the cartoons! Look, they have a screen. It's a sign, Billy." She looks at me pleadingly, and when I don't say anything she continues, "Why did we turn up at this tent at the perfect moment? How did we bump into sir?! Why did you happen to give your spare ticket to your techie who has all your tech stuff in his phone? Why are we even here in the first place? Because of your love of comedy. There are SO MANY SIGNS you should do this gig! You have to do it; you just have to!"

I hesitate. She seems so sure, and Blakemore is nodding enthusiastically. I take a big breath in.

"F-F-Fine!" I say. But Mr Osho can see that I am wavering.

"If you want to do this, Billy, you have to go for it. Fully commit. You know that comedy is not something you can do half-baked. Sometimes you have to behave as though you are feeling positive even if you aren't and that can trick your mind until it really is feeling positive. Think about it, Billy."

I think for a while. Do I always want to walk through the main entrance with the other festival-goers – or do I want to walk through the artists' entrance one day? Maybe Skyla is right. I can't give up after one bad gig.

I think about what Mr Osho said. "*Sometimes you have to behave as though you're feeling positive even if you aren't.*"

I stand up straight and put a big fake smile on my face.

"Let's do this!"

Skyla snorts. "Billy, you look weird."

"I'm fine!" I say through my fixed cheesy grin. "I'm positive! I can't wait!"

And all the while, terror is surging through my body.

CHAPTER 9

I broke up with my girlfriend by walkie-talkie.

She didn't get it no matter how many times I said it was over.

We find the lady with the walkie-talkie backstage where she is signing all the acts in and sorting the tech out. She tells us her name is Majeeda.

"How exciting!" she says when we remind her about me volunteering. "Thanks for stepping in. This will be something to tell everyone at school next week, won't it?"

When she's shown me where the toilets are and the entrance to the stage, I leave her talking to Blakemore about the tech, and me and Skyla go round the front of the tent to have another look at the stage from where the audience are.

"It's much b-b-bigger than the pub," I say nervously.

"Bigger and better," Skyla says firmly.

Blakemore joins us. "Tech's all ready," he says proudly. And then we go quiet because the act before me steps on to the stage.

The circus performer is a tall man with a beard who does juggling, magic tricks and rides a unicycle. The families seem to love him, but there are still lots of kids running around and people keep getting up and walking out like it's normal to leave halfway through a show. As I watch him juggling water balloons and pretending to eat them, I think that if *he* can't keep their attention, then surely a little kid stammering into a microphone has no chance.

Before my panic really sets in, the circus man starts saying goodbye and I need to be backstage so I dash round to Majeeda, who is waiting at the side of the stage for me. The circus man comes off with his unicycle. He is red-faced and sweaty and as he hands Majeeda the mic pack he mutters, "Tough crowd. I hate festival gigs," and walks off.

Majeeda gestures to the stage and I know that

there's no getting out of it: I have to put one foot in front of the other. I clutch my Granny Bread shells and move my feet. As I take my first step, my mouth goes completely dry. *Not this again.*

I turn back to Majeeda. "Have you got any water?!"

She quickly hands me a bottle and I take a huge mouthful. At least my mouth won't taste like a flip-flop for this gig, however badly it goes.

As I step out, I see that half of the tent has emptied. A band has started on the stage next to us and I can hear the thrum of the bass. I look out and see Skyla sitting on her coat next to Mr Osho. I remember the time I did my show-and-tell speech. It feels so long ago. I had worried I wouldn't be able to get a single word out. I remember their faces smiling at me as I held up my cardboard signs. They have been there for me from the beginning of this dream. So I smile and do it for them.

"G-G-G-G-G-G-Good afternoon, everyone." Oh no, that was a really big one. This could be bad. "My n-n-n-n-n-n-name is B-Billy Plimpton." A baby starts crying and some kids are playing tig at the back of the tent. I glance over to Skyla and Mr Osho. I need to focus on them. However weird it may be, I need them to keep looking back at me and smiling, otherwise I won't be able to do this. If I'm distracted by the family chatting and eating their picnic, or the couple asleep in the fold-out chairs, or the people who poke their heads into the tent and scowl at the sight of me, I'll run away. I need friendly faces.

I smile at them and they smile back. I know they're not going anywhere.

"Obviously my name is n-n-not B-B-Billy. It's just got the one B. That would have been cruel of my parents, wouldn't it? Name the kid with the stammer B-B-Billy, see how he copes."

I hear one person other than Mr Osho laughing and I take that as a good sign. The laugh is a low, rhythmical chuckle that's somehow familiar, but I don't risk looking away from my friends to see who it is. I take another sip of water and carry on.

"I n-n-normally open my gigs by juggling water balloons on a unicycle, but that's already been done, hasn't it?" I gesture offstage, towards where the circus man left. I hear the same low laugh from somewhere at the back of the tent but keep my eyes glued to the spot. Then I launch into my best joke book jokes and feel the safety that they offer me.

"Have you seen the ducks by the main stage?" I ask Skyla and Mr Osho. (There are no ducks at the main stage, but no one will know that. It's just a way to make my joke seem improvised or "off the cuff".) "They were super cute. They had these really long tail feathers. I think they have them to cover their butt quack." Skyla rolls her eyes and I see Mr Osho laugh. He's watching the screen behind me, which – if Blakemore is doing his job correctly – should now have a picture of me with a duck's body looking embarrassed and covering my bum with my feathery fingers.

The rest of the ten minutes seems to take for ever and even though I'm not looking around, I can feel the whole tent breathing, shuffling and chattering. After a pretty rubbish joke about a magician and a fisherman (pick a cod any cod) a couple of kids poke their heads around the entrance and shout, "Get off, you're rubbish!"

Time stands still. My first proper heckle. I know I can't ignore them – they were loud and clear enough for everyone to hear.

I have the perfect comeback ready. *"Next time someone offers you a penny for your thoughts. Sell!"* But my throat closes up and the words get stuck. All the audience can hear from me is, "N-N-N-N-N-N-N..." as the kids run away and my moment is over.

By the time I get to the end I'm exhausted. My last joke gets a pretty decent laugh and I hear the familiar chuckle again, but I'm too tired to appreciate the laughter. I take my bow to the sound of about seven people clapping and as I straighten up, feeling like this was yet another bad gig, I see him. He's wearing a cap low over his face, but I would recognize him anywhere.

Leo Leggett is standing at the back of the tent – CLAPPING!

I stand there for far too long, staring at him, until I hear Majeeda shout, "PSSST. Get off." As I stumble off the stage he disappears, leaving me wondering whether he was ever really there at all.

CHAPTER 10

I wanted to start my own rock group and call it The Rubber Band.

But I thought it was a bit of a stretch.

After the gig my head is buzzing. Blakemore and Skyla are talking, but I can't focus on anything they're saying. I keep going over everything that I said onstage. Reliving every second. Trying to remember the deep laugh in the audience. Had it come from Leo Leggett? Had he laughed at *my* jokes?

Blakemore keeps apologizing because one of the projections came up too late, but I tell him not to worry about it. None of that matters because Leo Leggett has seen me perform. I almost tell Skyla and Blakemore that he was there, but I stop myself.

They probably won't believe me, and I want to keep this to myself for a while longer. We go to the side of the stage and find an area that has a load of crisps and flapjack bars laid out for the artists. I'm suddenly ravenous and so grab a flapjack and shove it into my mouth greedily. As I am putting two bags of crisps into my pocket, Majeeda appears behind us.

"Billy," she says, and I jump out of my skin, thinking she's about to tell me off for taking too much of the free stuff. "Someone dropped this off for you." She hands me an envelope and then smiles and adds, "Enjoy the freebies; one of the perks of being famous, eh?"

"Not exactly famous," I say and then add with a wink, "yet."

I can feel a tiny spark of hope building inside me again. Even though the gig was hard, I did it. I even enjoyed a couple of moments during it. Maybe my career in comedy isn't over after all.

Skyla is yawning and rubbing her eyes. She still looks too pale and tired, I think. "You not going to open it? It could be a love letter from one of your adoring fans," she says.

I look down at the bulging envelope and peel open

the flap. When I open the letter and start to read, my face must go as pale as Skyla's.

"What is it?" she asks.

"You are n-n-n-n-not going to believe this," I say.

Blakemore stops shoving crisps into his mouth and turns to listen too. I hold up the letter and read it out.

"Dear Billy,

Leo saw your gig this afternoon and would like to invite you and a guest to watch his show from backstage.

He would love to meet you afterwards.

Best wishes,

Leo Leggett's team."

Inside the envelope are two guest lanyards.

"I'm going to meet Leo Leggett!"

"Wow, and I thought the tent was just full of tired parents and bonkers kids," Skyla says. "Who knew Leo Leggett was in there? Just shows you, I guess, that you always have to be on your game. You never know who's watching."

"I s-s-saw him," I say, still staring at the letter as though it might disappear.

"What? You saw Leo Leggett?" grunts Blakemore through a mouthful of crisps. "Why didn't you tell us?"

"He was wearing a hat. I c-c-couldn't quite believe it."

"Well, he must have liked what he saw." Skyla smiles. "Who you going to take?"

"You, of course."

Blakemore wipes his mouth and looks annoyed. "What about me?"

"Erm, it's just that Skyla has been my friend for a long time and…"

"Oh, here we go," he mumbles, looking upset. "You and her and The Regulars have got your little gang and I'm not part of it. I get it."

"Well, yeah," I say. "You are a great techie and I'm glad you're helping with the shows, but I've got to take Skyla. She's one of my best mates and I don't think she's ever tied me to a lamp post or punched me in the stomach."

I can't quite believe I have said this out loud. I've never said anything to Blakemore about how horrible he used to be. He could get angry and put me in a headlock or something, but instead he shrugs and looks at his shoes.

Skyla laughs. "There's still time, Plimpton. Watch your step. I might tie you to a lamp post at any minute!"

She winks, and Blakemore says, "Fine, I'll just watch from the front. It'll be a better view anyway."

"Anyway, that's not until later," I say, trying to think of something to cheer him up. "Aren't you dragging us to some unlistenable heavy metal now?"

"Yes!" he says and looks instantly happier. Then he takes off his hoodie to reveal a Metallica T-shirt and says, "Forget about boring old comedy. Let's go and rock out!"

As we follow him through the crowds, Skyla leans in and whispers, "He's not so bad, is he?"

"No," I admit. "If I'd said all that to him six months ago he would have had me in a headlock immediately."

As we get close to the rock stage we can hear the guitars screeching and see the sea of people all thrashing around, jumping up and down in waves. Blakemore immediately hurls himself in and me and Skyla look at each other, not knowing whether to be terrified or excited. We get sucked into the crowd. Then we grab on to each other's hands, smile and have no other choice but to start jumping.

After forty minutes in the mosh pit, a bit of Josh something strumming his guitar and singing love songs is just what we need. We flop down on the grass where we can see the stage but it's a bit less busy.

I can't stop looking at my watch. I feel sick and excited at the same time. I have always wanted to see Leo Leggett live – I can't even believe I'm going to do that later, let alone actually meet him. What if he hated my gig? But he wouldn't have invited me if he thought I was rubbish, would he? Will I get to speak to him? I want the time to go faster, but Josh-whoever-he-is drones on and on.

Lying on the grass, I start practising what I should say to Leo Leggett. I don't have a piece of paper on me, but I write an imaginary list in my head.

THINGS TO SAY TO LEO LEGGETT

1. You are the funniest person I've ever seen. (Maybe too suck-up. I need to play it cool.)
2. I loved the last episode of *The Leo Leggett Show*. The bit where you phoned your gran and pretended to be a turkey made my mum wee herself a bit, but then she's pregnant and

wees at everything. (Too much information? Not sure if you can start a conversation by talking about mum wee.)

3. Thanks for coming to see my show. Were you the one doing the cartwheels or the one asleep in a chair? (Good. Start with a gag. Talk about gigging as though you are both on the same level.)

4. Do you have any advice for me as a kid just starting out? (Good opener. Makes him feel important – although I imagine Leo Leggett always feels important.)

As I am sitting there on the grass trying to hold all of the options in my head, Skyla notices my scrunched-up expression. "What are you doing?"

"Just thinking about what to say to Leo Leggett."

"Ah, running through all the options?"

"Yup. M-Making a list."

"Of course. What you going to go for?"

"I think number three," I say thoughtfully.

"Strong choice. Three is my lucky number. Would you like to try it out on me?"

"No, thanks. I don't mind your eye-rolls for my jokes, but this is serious stuff."

"Well, me and my eye-rolls are here for you if you change your mind."

Blakemore rises up from where he has been sleeping next to me on the grass, like a bear coming out of hibernation. "Ah, is this not over yet?" he says, gesturing to the stage. It turns out that singer-songwriters expressing themselves about love are not up Blakemore's street.

"We'd better start heading over to the comedy tent anyway," Skyla says. "It'll be absolutely rammed."

We all pull each other up off the floor, pick up our coats and make our way towards what feels like it could be the most important meeting of my life.

Field Fest

CHAPTER 11

What do you call a famous turtle?

A shellebrity.

As we approach the comedy tent we can see the crowd spilling out from every entrance.

"It's a good job we've got backstage tickets," Skyla sings, waving her lanyard around. "Otherwise we wouldn't be able to see a thing!"

Blakemore scowls. "No need to rub it in."

"How about this?" Skyla says. "If you can answer the following question about Leo Leggett correctly, I will give you my pass."

Blakemore perks up. "Go on then!"

"What is Leo Leggett's dog's middle name?"

Skyla is looking smug. I know Blakemore won't

get it. Even I don't know the answer and I'm his biggest fan. I've seen all of his Amazon specials at least ten times; I pretty much know them off by heart. I watch his Saturday night show every single week and I've never heard him mention his dog's middle name.

Blakemore scrunches up his face as he thinks and then eventually says, "That's a stupid question. How should I know?"

"Ah, tough luck, Blakemore. See you after the show!" Skyla grabs my arm and we head towards the back of the tent where the artists' entrance will be. She is laughing to herself.

"What *is* Leo's dog's middle name?" I ask as we weave our way through hordes of people.

"No idea!" says Skyla, grinning.

"Ah, I almost feel sorry for him," I say, and she tips her head to the side and sticks out her tongue and then points up at the backstage sign. "Here we go, superstar."

After we show a huge man our passes, we step into the back of the tent. It's a lot like the tent where I performed, but about twenty times bigger. There are people buzzing about with walkie-talkies and clipboards. None of them even look at us. Then I hear someone talk into the microphone and we move towards the sound.

We can see everything from back here. The stage, the enormous crowd and a woman at the microphone who I think I've seen on a comedy panel show. She's introducing Leo.

"This man needs no introduction. Please start the drum roll. Use your feet, use your hands, use the head of the person in front of you." The whole tent starts throbbing with noise as people stamp and clap. "Please welcome to the stage, your headline act for the day, it's the one, the only, LEO LEGGETT!"

It feels like the tent is about to take off. The noise is incredible. I can see people in the audience screaming and whistling and shouting his catchphrase, "GET IN THE TOILET!" This is different to anything I've ever seen. It's miles away from the pub or the tent with the cartwheeling kids. This is what it feels like at the top. This is what I want. I want to see faces like that, waiting for me to appear. I want to hear people screaming my name.

As Leo Leggett steps on to the stage the whole tent screams even louder and he falls over backwards as though the noise has knocked him out. He does this every time he walks on to a stage: it's one of his "things". From where I'm standing I can see a mattress on the floor where he falls. I whisper and point it out to Skyla.

"I always wondered how he did that without hurting himself," she whispers back.

As he stands up, the screaming erupts for a second time and over he goes again. He's like a conductor, controlling the audience without even saying a word.

When he gets up after the third fall, he snatches the microphone and shouts, "Enough of that, you ridiculous people! I'm thirty-five, for goodness' sake, you'll kill me." Everyone laughs and the noise settles enough for the show to begin.

"I'll tell you something I've realized today. Festival bogs are disgusting." The audience cheer. "Festival bogs are so unbelievably revolting. Festival bogs can most definitely do one. What do we say to festival bogs, everyone?"

Before he has even finished his sentence the whole tent shouts as one, "GET IN THE TOILET!"

"Now that is a first," Leggett says. He struts confidently around the stage, owning every millimetre. "I have never before told an actual toilet to get in the toilet."

Everyone roars. I wonder if he even needs to

tell jokes; people seem programmed to find him hysterical whatever he says. It can't have been like that when he first started out, I think – doing gigs to half-empty tents, before everyone knew his catchphrase.

He launches into some material about taking his dog Wayne for a walk and pretends to be a dog having its bum sniffed and finding it disgusting. He ends up spinning around in circles shouting, "Stop sniffing my bum!" at the top of his voice. The crowd are loving it. I can see people crying and wiping their eyes. I remember my audience at the Bannerdale School talent show doing the same thing. I want to experience that feeling again.

After the gig the crowd go wild yet again and Leo takes a big bow and heads towards the side of the stage where we're standing. I try to quickly move out of his way, but I bump into Skyla and we both fall off the step we are standing on and land in a heap at Leo Leggett's feet.

He looks down and steps over us, reaching out for some water to be handed to him from someone with a walkie-talkie. I stumble to my feet. He's looking at us both with an expression of either confusion or disgust; I can't tell which.

Then one of the walkie-talkie people whispers something in his ear and his face changes.

"The boy from the tiny tent earlier! With your little friend. Welcome! Welcome, both!" He puts an arm around me and Skyla and walks us to a tented room with sofas. People are buzzing around him offering towels, drinks and chocolates as he sits down and stretches out on the sofa. Me and Skyla perch awkwardly on the other sofa.

"Pretty great show, eh?" Leo says. "I love festival gigs. So raw."

There is a gap, which I am clearly supposed to fill. I completely forget everything on my list of things to say and the first things that pops into my head fall out of my mouth in a jumble.

"You were God... I mean amaze... I'm... It's f-f-f-f-funny. M-Man." Skyla nearly chokes on her laughter. I instantly know that she will never let me forget these words.

Leo Leggett doesn't seem too bothered by me telling him that he is a god; maybe he's used to it. He just looks right at me and says, "Well, thank you. I think that you have something really special, kid. Don't get me wrong, you need work, but I can help with that. What do you say?"

"W-W-What do I say to w-w-w-w-what?" I ask.

"Oh, that stutter is so cute. People will totally fall for it. Can I ask you something? Billy, isn't it?"

"Y-yes?"

"Do you want to be a comedian? Really want it, I mean?"

I don't even think about it. "Of c-c-c-course I do," I say.

"Right, that has made my mind up. I'm posting." With that, Leo Leggett takes out his phone and taps away.

"Can I?" He holds up his phone with an image of me on the stage on it.

"Erm…"

"Do you want to be famous?"

"Yeah."

"OK then. Your wish is my command."

After a minute he looks up, shows me his phone and says, "Two million people have just been introduced to you on TikTok and Insta, young man. I hope you meant what you said."

"Yeah," I say, still not really knowing what has just happened.

"Right, well, I've got to skedaddle, but if you want to work on some material, get rid of those tacky joke book jokes and come up with some belters. I have an hour free every Wednesday. We can workshop ideas and take some pics for my socials." I look at Skyla and we both grin. "I'm fronting the government's big new anti-bullying campaign. They needed a real man of the people to get their message across, and of course I was only too happy to help, especially when the prime minister put a personal call in to me."

His assistant coughs politely behind us. "Yes, I'm coming. He is *perfect* for it. I can't believe I found him," he tells her, then turns back to me. "See you soon, kid. Yes?"

"Yes," I mumble, trying not to let out the squeal that has slowly been building inside me.

"That's what I like to hear!" He struts away, calling back over his shoulder, "See you Wednesday. One of my people will be in touch. Give them your parents' number. They'll send a car."

"OK!" I squeak.

"Your life is about to change, kid. I hope you're ready."

CHAPTER 12

How do you get straight As?

By using a ruler.

School is completely nuts. The minute I walk in the doors I'm surrounded by kids.

"Did you actually meet Leo Leggett?"

"What was he like?"

"Did he really laugh at your jokes?"

They are all holding their phones, and the fifteen-second video of me introducing myself onstage is playing over and over again. I'd had no idea that Leo Leggett had been filming my gig. If I'd realized at the time, I probably would have fallen off the stage.

The questions get more and more ridiculous.

"Is it true that Leo Leggett is your uncle?"

"Did you pay him to post the video?"

"Are you going on *The Leo Leggett Show*?"

I have not heard from Leo or "his people" yet, so I don't answer their questions. What if he's forgotten all about me?

Even the teachers can't help themselves. In drama, Miss Gallagher asks me all about it and then makes us do comedy routines inspired by Leo Leggett for the whole lesson. Only Mr Johnson seems the same as usual. He catches me signing someone's arm with a Sharpie and shouts that I would be straight in detention if it wasn't the last two days of school.

When he marches away, I giggle. Even he doesn't scare me any more. I'm famous and he knows it! If he gave me a detention, I could get Leo to tell the world about it. Then the world would hate Mr Johnson as much as I do. People had better not mess with me any more. My name is Billy Plimpton and I am an internet sensation!

Kids are staring at me in the hall, and at lunch everyone surrounds me again. I feel weird eating my sandwich while they're all looking at me and asking questions. I want to be famous, but I also want to eat my egg sarnie in peace!

After school I visit Mrs Gibbens with Scraggles. I show her my phone and try to explain what TikTok is.

"So, you put videos on it and people can like them or comment on them." I scroll through, showing her the moving stream of posts.

"Look, there I am," I say, pointing to Leo's video of me walking on to the stage.

"Oh, look at you. You look very handsome, Billy."

"Thanks," I say. As I watch, the likes keep on ticking up. "Leo Leggett posted it yesterday and it's already got thousands of likes and nearly a million views."

"Well, that sounds like a lot."

"It is. I've g-g-g-gone viral, Mrs Gibbens."

She pulls a face and moves away from me.

"It's a phrase! It means a lot of people are seeing this video."

"That's marvellous. Now can you get the cheese? Scraggles looks famished!"

I check my phone again. The likes are still building. It's hard to stop watching as the number ticks up. I move from TikTok to Twitter to YouTube and then Instagram, and it's happening on all of them.

Dad was not happy when he found out about the video. He was in a bad mood anyway because we were late to meet him at the family tent and I'd forgotten to text him every hour like I said I would. When I explained where I'd been he calmed down a bit but then when I told him that I was going to be a viral sensation, courtesy of Leo Leggett, he got really annoyed again.

"So, he didn't even ask your permission or tell you what he was going to post?"

"Yeah, he did ask. Stop worrying, Dad. L-L-Look, p-p-people are loving it! I thought my comedy career was over, but it's only just started. I am going to be huge!"

"I don't care. It's not OK to post videos of kids without checking with their parents first. I don't care how famous he is."

When we got home, I heard him and Mum talking for ages. I think they're still pretty cross.

When I get back this afternoon after dropping Scraggles off, Mum is lying on the sofa under her enormous bump. She's huffing and puffing now every time she has to stand up or sit down and is spending most of the time being propped up on the sofa by various cushions.

Cushions have become a thing with Mum. When I walk into the living room, she waves at me. "You can put some beans on yourself, can't you, Billy?" she says. "Sorry! It's the baby."

I start thinking about all the things she blames on the baby and decide to start a new list.

THE "IT'S THE BABY" LIST

1. Stealing all of the cushions in the house to wedge around herself – "It's the baby."
2. Crying for no reason whatsoever – "It's the baby."
3. Laughing for no reason whatsoever – "It's the baby."
4. Weeing herself when she is laughing or crying for no reason whatsoever – "It's the baby."
5. Eating all the ice in the freezer – "It's the baby."
6. Huffing, puffing, grunting and groaning – "It's the baby."
7. Buying secret packets of fizzy Haribos and not sharing them – "It's the baby."
8. Burping, yawning and farting at the dinner table – "It's the baby."
9. Interrupting every single conversation with, "Oh, it just kicked!" and then making me put my hand on the bump to feel ... absolutely nothing –"It's the baby."

Mum is a bit weird when she's pregnant. I hope she goes back to being Normal Mum when the baby comes. She can't keep blaming her annoying behaviour on the baby once it's born.

Imagine if your parents still blamed everything on you when you were grown up. If I'm sitting around the dinner table at Christmas with a family of my own and then Mum farts, rubs her belly and blames it on me, I will not be happy.

After tea, me and Chloe are having our usual argument over who gets to go on the iPad when Dad comes in holding his phone.

"So, your superstar friend has somehow found my phone number, Billy. Or his assistant Sal has, at any rate."

"I gave it to them."

"You did what?"

"What did she say?" I ask, dropping the iPad into Chloe's outstretched arms.

"He's inviting you to 'workshop your ideas', whatever that means. Along with his 'team'."

"W-What else does it say?"

"That a car will come at twelve o'clock on Wednesday."

"That's the first day of the holidays!" I say. "So

that's fine! You said I could do more comedy g-g-gigs in the summer!"

Dad is shaking his head. "Not so fast, Billy. I'm working and obviously Mum can't go."

"I'll just go on my own."

"I don't think so, Bill."

"Well, I'll get Skyla to come then. It's the holidays. You are not stopping me from d-d-d-doing this, D-Dad. Do you have any idea how big this is?"

He sighs. "What about Skyla's mum?"

"Erm no," I say, knowing that's never going to happen. Dad looks at me, waiting for an explanation.

"Skyla's mum's too busy, but there will be grown-ups there. Talk to Sal. It will be fine, Dad!"

"I'll think about it. But I'm going to speak to Leo – or one of his *team* – before I decide anything, OK?"

I nod, grab my phone to check the likes on Leo's video of me – 851,459 – and call Skyla. Her phone rings out. She wasn't at school today. I don't know if she even realizes that I'm now a viral superstar. I have texted her a constant stream of screenshots showing my views and likes, but she hasn't replied to any of them.

I look at Chloe lounging on one sofa on some stupid pony app and then Mum on the other sofa wrestling with a blanket and some cushions and decide to get out and go and knock for Skyla. I need to talk to someone who isn't pregnant or pony-obsessed. I need to tell Skyla that it's happening. She's coming with me to Leo Leggett's actual house! We will be treated like superstars. My summer of comedy is about to get bigger than I could ever have imagined. I can't believe I was ready to give up on it because of one rubbish gig in a grotty old pub. Turns out I was just too good for the King's Head.

On my way over to Skyla's, I'm sure that people are staring at me. Two little kids are whispering and I'm convinced they're talking about me. This must be what it feels like to be famous, always wondering if you're being recognized, never quite knowing if you can fully relax.

I check my likes as I walk, going in a loop from one platform to another. The numbers are changing so fast that I feel dizzy. I can't stop checking. I know I should, but I can't.

Skyla's street is pretty rough. I have walked her to the end of the road before and watched her go inside her house, but she's never invited me in. She lives about halfway down. The house on one side of hers has its curtains drawn and the house on the other has a garden full of rotten old cars with smashed windows. Skyla's house is sandwiched in the middle.

I push the rusty gate open and knock on the door. When Skyla looks out of the front window and sees me, I know straight away that something is wrong.

Very wrong.

CHAPTER 13

Why are skeletons always scared?

They have no guts.

The front door opens a crack. Skyla's blotchy red face peeks out of the gap.

"What are you doing here?" she hisses.

"You weren't answering," I say, holding up my phone.

"You've got to go. NOW." But just as she finishes saying it, I hear her mum in the background. She's shouting and there's something weird about her voice.

I've only met Skyla's mum once before. Me and Mum bumped into them on our way into town ages ago. Skyla went really red and shy – I'd never seen her like that before. Her mum didn't say much and seemed a bit confused when my mum started suggesting that she pop over for a coffee.

"Seeing as the kids are so close, it seems daft that we've never met!"

But Skyla looked horrified at the idea, and her mum just kept her head down. Skyla has never invited anyone to her house; she always comes to ours. She draws ponies for Chloe and always clears the table after tea. Mum says sometimes it feels like she has another daughter, but one who actually helps around the house. Since that time on the bus, Mum always asks Skyla how her mum is and Skyla always just smiles and says, "Fine thanks," and then quickly changes the subject.

Skyla quickly tries to close the door, but her mum appears behind her and grabs the handle. She looks different from the time we bumped into her on the bus; her hair is messy and I think she's wearing pyjamas. Her head is not down now, and she doesn't seem quiet at all.

"Who is your little pal, Sky?" she says in a loud, strange, slurred voice. "Is it your boyfriend?"

Skyla looks at me and whispers, "Go. Please go now."

I don't know what to do. Her mum opens the door

a bit wider and a smell hits me. Like sick and vinegar. Behind them both I see into the house and it's like they've been burgled. There is a chair on its side and the floor is littered with cans and plastic bags.

"What's happening, Skyla?" I ask.

"Leave me alone, Billy," she says and then she turns and walks away into the house.

Her mum looks at me through slitted eyes, "YEAH, BILLY WHOEVER YOU ARE, YOU HEARD HER…" Her voice is full of hate.

I turn and run back through the gate and up the road. I hear the door slamming behind me.

I keep running all the way home and when I get there I stand outside, out of breath, wondering what it is that I have just seen.

The only other time I've seen someone look and sound like Skyla's mum was at the train station when Dad took me to London. A homeless man was shouting at everyone who walked past. My dad said he wasn't well and that it was really sad. But that was a homeless person in London – that can't happen to mums in houses, can it?

I know Skyla's mum was sad because of the baby who died, but today she didn't look sad. She looked angry and scary. I don't know what to do. I never want to go back to that house again. I keep picturing the terrified look on Skyla's face. I think about all the stupid texts I've been sending her about my new-found fame. No wonder she didn't reply. I feel guilty and embarrassed too. How could I not have realized how bad things were? But then she never tells me anything so how am I supposed to know what's going on? This all feels too big and grown up for me to deal with.

Just as I'm deciding if I should tell Mum and Dad, or if I should go back and knock again, my phone starts buzzing, Skyla's name flashing up on the screen.

"Skyla, are you OK?" I say when I answer it.

"Yeah, I'm fine!" she laughs, as though what I've just seen didn't even happen. "Ignore my mum, she's so annoying. I can't believe that the video has blown up, you must be so pleased."

We both know she's pretending.

"D-D-D-Do you want to come over? Until your mum calms down."

"It's fine, Billy. Don't say anything to your parents, OK?"

I pause and she carries on. "You know what mums are like: they get a bit shouty. One of her bad days, that's all. She'll be fine tomorrow. I'll be back at school. How was it today? Has everyone seen the video?" She sounds more normal now. Maybe I *did* overreact. Maybe it wasn't as bad as I thought.

"Yeah," I say. "It was pretty full-on. Have you seen how many likes Leo's post has had? Wait, that reminds me!"

I tell her how Leo Leggett's people have been in touch and ask her to come and she says "definitely". Everything feels safe and normal again until we are saying goodbye and she says, "Thanks, Billy. Look, promise me you won't mention Mum being cross today to anyone, will you?"

"OK," I say, not really knowing what else I can say.

She sounds relieved. "It's a bit embarrassing, that's all. Imagine if I told everyone about your mum crying and weeing herself all the time!"

I hesitate, then say, "Yeah, sure." But as I hang up I know that my mum being a bit embarrassing and her mum being how she was today are not the same thing at all.

The scary thing is, I have absolutely no idea what to do about it.

CHAPTER 14

Why did the echo get detention?

It kept answering back.

It's the last day of term today. Skyla is back at school, like she said she would be, and she seems OK. I'm not sure if she's just pretending for my sake, though. I'll have to keep an eye on her.

At lunch we chat about Leo Leggett.

"How many times do you think you will tell him that he is a god tomorrow, Billy?" Then she makes her hands into a heart shape and puts on a silly, whiny baby voice. "I wuv you SO much, Leo Leggett."

"Shut up, that was an accident." I say, feeling my cheeks burning up. She laughs and throws a chip at me.

"So what time are we leaving? Will it be a limo

115

or something? It had better be a fancy car with free snacks, that's all I'm saying."

"Shall I tell them that we will only come if we get free snacks?"

"Too right. You're famous, Plimpton, start making your demands."

School is weird now. The likes on the video are still ticking up and it feels like the whole world knows who I am now. There are even memes and GIFs of me. The teachers have completely given up on any teaching and so my time today has been spent doodling and chatting and generally being surrounded by people asking me a million questions about being famous. When it gets too much or any of the jealous kids start saying mean stuff, Blakemore always appears and tells people to leave me alone, and no one messes with Blakemore. He's like my bodyguard.

Being famous isn't as exciting as I thought it would be. It's only one video and it's all online and so nothing feels very real. Someone took a picture of me at the supermarket yesterday – but it was actually kind of annoying.

First off, I was in a mood with Mum because she wouldn't let me get any Coco Pops.

"It's pure sugar, Billy. Not a good way to start the

day and with my hormones I'll just end up stealing it anyway. It's the baby."

I had grumpily put the cereal back on the shelf mumbling, "It's always the baby," under my breath and making a mental note to add it to the list. I had turned round to find someone holding their phone up in front of my face. I'm pretty sure I didn't look funny or cool. I probably looked like a spoilt little kid being horrible to a heavily pregnant lady – not a good look.

I guess I could try and always look happy in public places in case it ever happens again, but that sounds pretty exhausting to me.

Finally, the bell rings, marking the end of the day and the end of term! Some of the girls start to go all weird, hugging and pretending to cry. I think they just love the drama. It's only six weeks and if they love each other so much they will see each other anyway. When I say goodbye to The Regulars we have an awkward handshake/high five that nearly turns into a hug but doesn't.

I never know when the right time is to handshake/hug/high-five. I think it should be clearer – which one to do when. There should be proper rules in place. I think a list would help – lists always help.

BILLY PLIMPTON'S RULES OF HUGS, HIGH FIVES AND HANDSHAKES

1. HUGS: Always hug family. Although, come to think of it, I never hug Chloe, I never hug Mum as she's massive and it would make her cry, and I never hug Dad. So maybe this should be NEVER hug family – apart from aunties and uncles at Christmas, but only if you know them quite well and want to hug them. Hug friends when they are crying – unless you are at school, in which case never hug anyone ever or you will never hear the end of it.

2. HANDSHAKES: Handshakes are for family members that you don't really know, who wear suits. Once Dad's cousin came to visit and he wore a suit and shook me by the hand. It made me feel very grown up. I tried to shake Dad by the hand the next time he was going to work and wearing a suit and he laughed at me. Occasionally teachers do a handshake. Mr Horter, our supply English teacher, gives out a "Horter Handshake" whenever you do especially good work. I

think he stole the idea off a baking show. I like handshakes – they feel important. Never attempt a handshake when greeting a friend; they will call you a weirdo.

3. HIGH FIVES: A bit childish in my opinion. Adults who think they are "down with the kids" like to offer up a high five but I always find it a bit patronizing. The only way kids can get away with it is the high-five-handshake hybrid, where you go in for a low high five and move seamlessly into a handshake. It can even be developed into a pull-in-and-back-slap if you want to take it further, but knowing when to unleash that can be tricky. I would suggest saving it for moments of excitement and joy with good friends.

To be honest I'm not sure if this list has made things clearer or not.

Anyway, The Regulars all say goodbye to each other. We've not been doing much rehearsing the last few weeks. I think it's because there is nothing to practise for. If we had a gig lined up then that would be different, but there isn't much call for a bad jazz band made up of kids. Anyway, I feel like I might be about to get far too busy to think about music for a while.

Alex looks fed up, as though he knows what I'm thinking.

"You are going to have the best summer ever and I am stuck with my family in a tent for a month."

"Shall I send you pics of me and Skyla at Leo Leggett's house or will that make it worse?"

"Far worse, but do it anyway," he says. I look at his face and make a decision and give him a full low high-five-hand-grab-pull-in-back-slap combo and then say my goodbyes to Josh and Matthew.

On the bus I stare out of the window and think about how much my life has changed. How much I have changed. When I started at Bannerdale I literally couldn't speak. I couldn't go anywhere near a stage. Now I'm famous for standing on a stage and saying my name. And it all began with a show-and-tell presentation.

CHAPTER 15

I spent all my pocket money renting a limo and it didn't even come with a driver.

I wasted all that money and I've got nothing to chauffeur it.

Leo Leggett does send a fancy car. It's not a limo with snacks, but it is an electric car with a nice smell and TVs in the back of the seats, so Skyla and I are pretty happy. I remember what Leo said about getting rid of my joke book jokes. What else will I have to work with? I think back to the talent show and remember all the impressions and other stuff I did. Maybe Leo will think that I should do more material like that. At the pub gig and the festival, it was the stuff about me or about the weirdness of the gig itself that got a laugh or two. Maybe I need to write more stuff like that; hopefully Leo will teach me how.

I really want him to think I'm funny. It's hard to be funny when you try too hard, though, so I am doing my counting breathing in the back of the car, watching the countryside turn into city, trying not to think about it all too much.

When we eventually pull up at a tall house with lots of windows, a short lady with wide eyes that look too big for her glasses comes and shows us in through the shiny black door and into a swanky living room.

"I'm Sal, Leo's assistant. I spoke to your Dad. Come on in. Leo will be with you in a minute. Take a seat. Can I get you a drink? Tea? Coffee? Juice?"

I've never been offered tea or coffee before by a grown-up and it almost makes me laugh out loud. Skyla and I both ask for some juice and she goes off to find some.

"I like this chair," whispers Skyla, stroking the velvet armchair that she's sitting in and looking around the grand hallway with photographs of Leo and lots of famous people covering the walls.

"It's pretty fancy, isn't it? Do you think he's got a pool? Maybe we should have brought our swimmers."

"You are here to write jokes, Billy, not do bombs

in someone's pool. Anyway, you can't have a pool in a townhouse – however fancy it is."

Then I hear voices and shush her. The door is slightly ajar so we can hear them – it's Leo talking to Sal.

"Sal, talk to Adrian, he needs the info for the Apollo Live gig." He lowers his voice, but we still just about hear. "This nonsense all *has* to blow over, Sal. I am not letting my career be ruined by this. Thank goodness for the kid, eh? Something to distract the press with at least."

Skyla and I look at each other, but before we can say anything, the doors swing open and Leo Leggett is in front of us. I wonder why Leo wants to distract the press. It sounds complicated. Maybe I will have paparazzi waiting outside my house soon and will need to think of ways to stop them hounding me. Poor Leo, it must be hard being so famous.

"Well!" Leo booms. "How does it feel to be a superstar?"

I giggle nervously and then Sal brings in the juice. It's in two tall glasses full of ice and fruit with straws sticking out of the top. Skyla and I grin at each other. Leo carries on talking, his booming voice makes Sal jump out of her skin, nearly spilling the juice as she passes it to us. She smiles apologetically and quietly sits down next to us.

"OK, I'm gonna be straight with you, kid. Are you ready?" I nod, eyes fixed on his. "You've got something special. There, I've said it." I feel a warm glow spread through me at his words, but Leo is still going. "It doesn't mean it's going to be plain sailing, though. No one said this was easy – and I'm going to give you some honest feedback." I gulp, waiting to hear what he has to say. "You have to ditch the joke book jokes and come up with some new material. Think about what makes *you* tick, are you up for it, Billy?"

I hope I can do what he thinks I can do. I reach into my pocket and clutch my shells, imagining what Granny Bread would say. *"Just be your gorgeous self, boy. That's all you have to do."*

I nod and Leo takes a phone out of his pocket and shows me the picture of a microphone on the screen. He hits the big red record button. "I record everything. So that we can capture the gold," he says. "Tell me about yourself, kid. Who are you? What's going on in your life? You see, to be a great comedian you need to figure out who you really are."

"W-W-W-Well…"

"First of all," he interrupts, "the stammer is great. Definitely keep it."

"I d-d-don't have m-much choice," I say.

"Funny! See? You are a very funny kid. So apart from the stuttering thing, which is obviously great, what else is happening?"

I want to tell him that I'm not doing it on purpose, it's not just part of my act, but he's looking at me keenly, waiting for more.

"W-W-Well, I'm a schoolk-k-k-k kid," I say.

"Yup. State or private?"

"State," I say.

"Great, perfect, state is much better. Far too many posh private-school kids coming into comedy anyway. What about your family?"

"I've got a sister called C-C-Chloe. My dad's a c-c-c-c-cameraman."

"Don't mention the cameraman thing – could sound like nepotism, ha ha. What else?"

I have no idea what *nepotism* means, but later when I look it up, I find out that it's something to do with getting a job because of who your family are.

"Well, my mum's p-p-pregnant ... REALLY p-p-p-p-p-p," I say.

Skyla can see that I'm stuck and rescues me.

"What about the list? Tell him about that." Skyla loves my lists. Whenever she comes over she always goes straight to my pinboard to see if there are any new ones on it.

I hesitate and she carries on. Sometimes in certain situations it is quite nice when someone does the talking for me and this is definitely one of those times.

"He's totally obsessed with writing lists and one of them is all about the things his mum does when she's pregnant – it's so funny." Hearing Skyla say how funny I am makes me feel better. I instantly relax enough to join in.

"It's called the IT'S THE B-BABY list because whenever Mum does anything annoying or anti-social she says, 'It's the baby.'" Leo looks interested in this, so I tell him all about it and mention everything on the list. He laughs at some of the things.

When I'm finished he claps his hands and says, "Brilliant. Such a cute story. I don't think it's strong enough for the stage, though. Tell me about school."

I sigh. I thought he might like my "It's the baby" list. I should have known it wouldn't be good enough for a professional comedian. What makes me laugh in my bedroom is very different to what will make Leo Leggett and the rest of the world laugh.

We chat for another half hour or so and I tell Leo about Shouty Man and he starts properly laughing. "That's it, kid!" he says at last. "You really are special. Keep it unique. You are the youngest schoolkid comic out there, so if you do school material then no one else will be doing it." Then Sal gives Leo a little nod.

"OK, that's it, folks. I've got a meeting, but I hope this has been helpful. And it is just the start, Billy. I want to help you – if you're keen?"

His eyes meet mine, and I nod so hard my head almost falls off. He grins.

"Don't worry, I won't demand a cut of your profits!" He stands and sweeps out of the room. As we follow after him, he turns, holding his phone. "Ooh, I forgot, quick selfie?" He stands between us and snaps a picture, then he's gone.

In the car home, Skyla and I are silent. It was amazing to go to Leo's house and exciting to see him again but Skyla has a funny look on her face. Eventually she leans over and whispers, "He's not as nice as I thought he'd be."

"Shhhhh!" I glance at the driver, terrified he might overhear us and tell Leo how horrible and ungrateful we are.

"What are you talking about? He was great!" I

whisper. "Anyway, people can't be exactly like they are on telly. We should be buzzing. How many twelve-year-olds can say they have been to Leo Leggett's house? Besides, he was really helpful."

"OK," says Skyla. "If you say so." I open my phone to check my likes and comments and a notification pings up.

"Look!" I say, holding up the phone. The picture of us smiling with Leo Leggett is staring out at us. I read the caption. "Best writing day ever with the world's next comedy superstar. Maybe we should do a double act now – before he gets too famous! #Kindercampaign #SayNoToBullying."

"See, he's *really* nice!" I say, grinning from ear to ear.

Skyla doesn't look convinced. "Mmm, nice online maybe … not so much in real life."

I barely hear her – I'm too busy watching my notifications flood in. "He's literally making me famous, Skyla! Look at the likes!" And I sit grinning as my fame keeps on growing.

CHAPTER 16

What do you call a plastic bird that steals?

A robber duck.

The next day a huge tray of brownies arrives at the door. They are stacked in a pyramid and there is a big blue bow on the top. The card says:

Thanks for a great writing session.
Leo Leggett

They are the most delicious brownies I have ever eaten. So gooey. I even give Chloe one because there are far too many for me to eat. As I tuck into my fourth, I smile to myself. I love my new life as a famous comedy superstar. Getting picked up in fancy cars and visiting famous people. Being sent stuff through the post. I never got huge pyramids of brownies before I was an internet sensation.

I need to make the most of it. Come up with some new jokes and get some more gigs booked in. I wonder if I could sell out an arena now that I'm famous. Imagine my face on a huge screen at the O2. Thousands of people staring up at it, crying with laughter.

I need some more jokes, though – Leo told me to stop using the old joke books. I'd hoped that I might come away from the session with Leo with a few more ideas, but I guess being a comedian is about coming up with the jokes yourself. Nobody else can do it for you, can they? I look up at my shelf full of joke books and feel a bit sad that I can't use them any more. They have been good friends. I read them when I'm bored or sad or just when I want to smile. I bet I know every single joke in every single book off by heart. I wonder if Leo Leggett has any joke books at home.

I fill a bag of brownies for Mrs Gibbens and head out to get Scraggles. The Thompsons needed extra help walking Scraggles and, as it's the summer holidays, I said I would do it. They're paying me, and

Mrs Gibbens is thrilled with the extra visits. She'll get to feed Scraggles even more than usual.

Walking a dog is good thinking time. I try out some new ideas on Scraggles, stuff about being a schoolkid like Leo said, and even though he can't laugh he seems to know when the punchlines are, and he cocks his head up at me and wags his stumpy little tail.

I never stammer when I talk to Scraggles. I think it's because there is literally zero chance of being judged or interrupted. Today when I run out of ideas I tell him all about Leo Leggett.

"He said it was the best writing session ever!" Scraggles looks at me. "He's my hero. He made me nervous and my stammer got bad, but that's just because he's so famous. Can you believe it, Scraggles? Leo Leggett! What do you think about that, eh?" Scraggles tilts his head and seems to think about it. Then he squats and does a massive poo.

"Well, that's not very nice, Scraggles!" I say as I prepare a bag.

When we get to Mrs Gibbens's room, Scraggles runs in like he always does and I flop down on the sofa. The TV is flickering with no sound, pictures of shiny people advertising things and cars whizzing around mountains.

After a few minutes, I go to the kitchen to get some juice and a cup of tea for Mrs Gibbens.

When the kettle is boiling, she calls, "Don't forget your choccy orange." Then she adds, "Oh, Billy, isn't that your famous friend on the telly?" I look around the corner at the TV and see Leo Leggett walking on to a huge stage in front of a massive audience. As he's doing his falling-over trick, I look for the remote.

"Can we turn it up?"

Mrs Gibbens turns the volume up and I can hear his voice.

"… and gentleman. I've got some new material for you tonight, folks. No one in the world has heard what I am about to tell you this evening. Straight from the funny factory," he says, tapping his brain.

"About time he did something new," Mrs Gibbens says. "All he ever does is fall over and say put it in the bin."

"It's 'Get in the toilet'," I say, smiling and turning back to the screen.

"Big news in our family," he says. "And when I say big, I mean BIG." As he says this, he gestures with his hands over his tummy, making it look round. Making it look pregnant. The audience whoop and cheer. I sit on the sofa, my mouth wide open as he continues.

"Yes, there is a baby on the way in the Leggett house and don't I know it? My wife is now constantly crying, burping and farting." He does an impression of someone doing all three and the audience howl. "But apparently it's not *her* doing all these things, ladies and gentlemen. No, *she* isn't sneeze-farting and crying at adverts – it's the baby!" He pauses after this and the audience know it's time to laugh again.

I am so confused. Leo didn't mention that his wife was pregnant when we were there. I didn't even know he had a wife. Before I can gather my thoughts, he carries on. "She's stolen every single cushion in the whole house, furiously wedging them underneath her." Then he gets on to the floor and mimes writhing around and wrestling with imaginary cushions while farting and crying. I'm not sure what to think, but I have to admit it's pretty hilarious. The audience are loving it. I look at Mrs Gibbens and she's stroking Scraggles. As he gets up off the floor, dusting himself off, he says, "Obviously *she* hasn't stolen the cushions has she, ladies and gentlemen? *She* hasn't stolen them! Who has? It's the baby, of course!"

He goes through all the items on my list and by the end of the show the entire audience are screaming along with him: "IT'S THE BABY!"

I stare at the screen, feeling numb and bewildered. He was saying it a bit differently, but surely most of that was mine. Leo can't have stolen all that from me, can he? He said it wasn't strong enough for material. No, that's ridiculous. Why would he do that? He's a famous comedian; he wouldn't need to steal a stupid list off a kid. But it can't be a coincidence, can it?

I'm still staring in shock, unable to speak, when Mrs Gibbens turns the TV off and says, "Well, at least he's got a new catchphrase."

CHAPTER 17

I hate Russian dolls.

They're so full of themselves.

After dropping Scraggles off, I head straight to Skyla's. I keep texting and calling her phone, but she's not answering. The image of Leo Leggett shouting his/my catchphrase into the delighted audience is replaying over and over in my head. Was that the only reason he invited me over? So that he could use my stories?

Just then my phone lights up. Private number.

"H-H-H-H…" I begin.

"Billy!" I recognize Leo's voice instantly. "How is my little comedy partner?"

"G-G-G-G—"

"Marvellous. The material we worked on together went down brilliantly at the Apollo, did you see it?"

"Y-Y-Y—"

"Wasn't it great? It's going through the roof on all the socials, as are you, kid. Knew you had what it took. Chatted to my manager and we thought it would be perfect timing to get you out onstage with me, launch us into the world as a double act, eh? Before that, though, there is an awards ceremony tomorrow night and guess who's coming with me? That's right! All the info will be sent to your dad. Anyway, got to go, Billy. Congratulations, kid."

The call ends and I stand there in silence for a while. What on earth just happened? My brain is whirring as I walk down the street. Maybe this is just how it works when you are a professional comedian? If you do a writing day together maybe both of you get to use the material, regardless of who actually said it first? I take the little bottle of shells out of my pocket and give it a squeeze.

"Is this OK, Granny Bread?" I whisper. "Leo using my 'It's the baby' list is no different to me using joke book jokes, is it?" I wait for an answer that doesn't come so I eventually carry on. "You hear people telling jokes from books all the time, and they never say who actually wrote them. Who came up with 'Why did the chicken cross the road?' No idea – they're never credited!"

I'm almost convincing myself, but something still feels off, so I keep going until I have a thought that I like. "I probably would never have thought to use the 'It's the Baby' stuff onstage anyway if I hadn't been to his house and talked about it, would I? And he did it so well." I smile and squeeze the shells, deciding that everything is OK. "It's all fine, isn't it, Granny Bread? AND I get to go to some awards AND go onstage with Leo!"

When I reach Skyla's road I shudder, thinking about the last time I was here. I almost turn round; even being on this street scares me. I wonder if it's a good idea to knock on the door again unannounced. But it must be – she said her mum was just a bit over the top last time. I tell myself it's OK and keep walking. Before I even get to the house, I see the door is wide open. When I peer inside it looks dark and scary. Bottles and food wrappers litter the floor and there is a lamp tipped on to its side.

"Hello?" I call quietly. "S-S-Skyla?" No one appears, so I step in through the open door. The smell is horrible, just like the last time I was here.

Vinegary and rotten. I walk through the sad, empty hall to the stairs, which are littered with dirty clothes. I think about all the times that Skyla said she's fine and I chose to believe her. I should have known that everything was not fine.

As I step over an empty takeaway box, I feel guilt flood my body. I've been so wrapped up in my own life that I just found it easier to believe what Skyla told me.

I climb the stairs a little faster. I can't believe Skyla lives like this. It feels like a horror movie: dark, damp and silent. Like something terrible is about to jump out at me at any moment.

"Skyla?" I call up the stairs. Still nothing. I take my phone out and try her again. I can hear her phone ringing from upstairs and follow the sound until I am standing outside what must be her bedroom. I almost can't do it. I'm not sure what I'll find on the other side of the door, but with a big breath I knock. Nothing. Another deep breath and I push the door open to find Skyla sitting in the corner of her room, scrunched into a tiny ball.

She has headphones on, and I can hear the thrum of music spilling out from them. Her eyes are tight shut and her phone is ringing out next to her. She hasn't heard it. When I go to her and gently touch her shoulder, she screams, which makes me scream, and for a second, we scream into each other's faces until she recognizes me and pulls her headphones off.

"What are you doing, Billy?!" she yells.

"W-W-What are *you* doing? What's going on, Skyla? Are you OK?"

"Is she gone?"

"Who?"

"Mum."

"There's no one downstairs and the front door was wide open. Are you OK?"

"Let's get out of here, Billy."

Skyla stands up and grabs me by the arm, pulls me back through the door and down the stairs.

Once outside we walk and walk. She doesn't let go of my arm and we keep walking, not saying a word.

Eventually, when we get to the park, we go in and I sit down on the bench. Skyla walks over to the pond, and I watch as she hugs her arms around her mouth and screams. The sound is muffled, but the pain is clear. The ducks all fly away and she keeps screaming into her arm.

I'm frightened. I feel completely out of my depth and don't know if this is the time for a hug or not.

There is nothing on my list of rules about whether hugging is appropriate when your best friend is screaming by a duck pond.

I think about when I'm struggling with my speech and that sometimes it's just best to wait. Maybe Skyla just needs to scream without interruption. Eventually she comes and sits next to me.

"I'm definitely not going to ask if you're OK again," I say, looking straight ahead.

"Good," she whispers.

We sit like that, side by side – staring ahead for ages, and then she whispers again, "I will tell you, Billy. I promise." She doesn't sound like the Skyla I know. It's like she's smaller, somehow. She keeps breathing in as though she's about to say something and then stops. "I'm finding it hard to speak," she says.

"I know all about that," I say.

"Can you talk to me first? Tell me something, anything. Then I will try again, I promise."

I think about what I came to tell her, and it feels so unimportant now. So trivial in comparison. Maybe trivial is what she needs, though, and so I talk. I tell her about the show and about Mrs Gibbens thinking Leo's catchphrase was "Put it in the bin" instead of

"Get in the toilet". Then I tell her about the "It's the baby" list and how the audience howled with laughter and how they shouted Leo's new catchphrase back at him. The whole time I'm talking I can feel Skyla slowly coming back. When I finish telling her about the Apollo show, she looks furious.

"We're going to take him down," she says.

"That's not the end of the story, Skyla. It t-turns out that actually it's OK that he used the list – m-m-m-more than OK, it's great!"

"What are you on about? He stole your—"

"N-No, he didn't! He just called me. Like, literally phoned me on my phone! He said that he wants me to be in a d-double act with him, Skyla, can you believe it?!"

"But he still stole your—"

"No, th-that's just how it works. We worked on it *together,* so it's fine that he used it. Anyway, it doesn't matter. I am going onstage with him and to an award ceremony! I can tell my own jokes to millions of people, Skyla. It's happening. Everything I had ever imagined is actually happening. I'm g-g-going to be famous!"

She looks at me, head down, eyes slitted. "I don't know about this, Billy."

"Oh, p-please just be happy for me, Skyla."

"Mmmm," she says, still not convinced.

"Anyway, I've d-d-done my talking. Now it's your turn," I say. "What's going on, Skyla?"

She shrinks a little bit and her voice goes smaller again, but she does it. She finds the words to tell me. She tells me about how her mum drinks, that she drinks until she laughs and dances and then drinks more until she shouts and screams and then more until she's sick and then sleeps. She tells me how it can stop, how her mum once gave up for a whole year, but that usually she gives up for a week or most often a day. How every time her mum says she's stopping, Skyla can't help but be hopeful. How she always feels like she will never hope again but then somehow manages to.

"I didn't know there was this much hope inside me," she whispers. "I wish there wasn't. It's the hope I hate. I hate it." She spits the last words. "That's what makes it so hard."

"I guess that's what keeps us going, though, isn't it?" I say. "Where would we be without hope?"

"I wouldn't be screaming by a chuffing duck pond, would I?"

We sit in silence again for a while. I turn to look

at her and I see tears silently streaming down her face. I have never seen Skyla anywhere near crying. Not when kids were cruel to her in primary. Not when she missed the next rung on the monkey bars and broke her arm. She's always so tough. But this Skyla is someone different, someone new. Her body shudders as though there is too much sadness inside to come out.

"I don't know what to do any more, Billy," she sobs. "I thought I could make her better. That I had to just try harder or be there at the right moment or make her prouder." A huge sob comes out. "I don't think I can, though. She's broken and I can't fix her."

I take her hand and hold it tightly in mine. It feels right. I don't need a list to know that. She holds on tightly and we stay that way until my hand gets sweaty and it starts getting dark.

CHAPTER 18

Two TV aerials met on a roof and got married.

The wedding wasn't very good, but the reception was fantastic.

I try and get Skyla to come home with me, but she won't. "She'll be back and asleep on the sofa by now," she says as we turn up her road. "I know the routine. I need to be there in case she's sick in her sleep. That's the thing that scares me most. What if I'm not there and she needs me?"

"You shouldn't have to do this, Skyla. It's a grown-up job."

"There are no grown-ups, Billy."

"Could you try and get hold of your dad?"

She snorts. "He's never been around, you know that. He certainly isn't going to rock up twelve years later and save the day."

"Surely there's someone?"

"Nope, there's only me. It's fine. I'm used to it." She shrugs then turns to face the quiet house.

All of the screaming into her arm and the crying is over. Skyla has gone back to how she was before.

I want to shout at her that it's not fine. Shake her and say that it's a long way from being fine. That no one should have to live like this. But I don't think it will make anything better, so I don't.

"I think we should make a plan," I say instead.

"What kind of a plan?"

"A plan for how to help you."

"I'm a lost cause, Plimpton, you should know that by now. Let's meet up tomorrow anyway." She lets herself into the house. I feel completely helpless as I stand there and watch the door close behind her.

When I walk through our front door, my mum is pacing around the kitchen holding her back. I don't know why she holds her back so much when the baby is very much taking up all the space round her front.

"Where on earth have you been, Billy? We were

worried sick. Don't tell me you didn't have your phone because you are glued to that thing."

Then I realize that they think I've been out walking Scraggles. I look down at my screen and see the missed calls. Talking to Skyla is the first time I have not been constantly checking my phone.

"I'm sorry. Skyla had an emergency," I say. Hoping that she's too tired to bother with a lecture. I hate Mum's lectures. I preferred it when I was younger and she would just tell me off and take away screen time or pudding, but recently she does this annoying thing of saying that I'm too old for telling off and instead she wants to "discuss it like adults". If that's how adults discuss everything I don't want to grow up. It's so boring talking about responsibility and communication all the time. I came in late, how about I say sorry, and you don't let me have ice cream tomorrow, rather than getting me to describe how I think it has made you feel "as a human being"? Or working out "mutual boundaries" that make us all happy.

She's thinking about what to say and then the baby kicks and distracts her. (I must remember to thank it when it comes out.) She strokes her bump and sighs and says that she's going to bed.

When Dad walks into the kitchen he doesn't say anything about where I've been. Instead, he holds up his phone and says, "I'm like your PA, Billy Plimpton." I have no idea what a PA is. Images of what the letters could stand for pop into my brain, forming an instant list, but none of them seem right:

1. Pine Apple
2. Personal Aardvark
3. Power Aimer
4. Proud Angel

He carries on, interrupting my internal list-making.

"Two invitations today. I'm not sure I want all these people messaging me."

"I'm pretty famous, Dad, people need to be able to reach me."

"All right, all right, Justin Bieber."

"Dad, you are so old!"

After grabbing me into a wrestle hold to prove his youth, Dad tells me about the award ceremony that Leo mentioned. It's the British Comedy Awards tomorrow; they are massive! Every comedian in the country will be there. As I am making a mental list of who I might see, Dad carries on reading the message.

I'm being picked up in a car and they are sending me a suit to wear!

"When you have finished swanning around with all your famous friends, you might be able to squeeze in another event... Now this one I think you will be very excited about." Then he winks and passes me his phone.

Dear Billy,

Everyone at *Morning Live Kidz!* has seen your video and we love you! We wondered if you would want to come on the show next Saturday and talk about your stand-up comedy experiences?

Leo Leggett will also be on the show and has expressed a wish that you both be on the sofa together.

Please let us know and we will call your parents to arrange.

Thanks,

The Morning Live Kidz! Team X

"Oh my god," I say and then do a little dance around the kitchen. "Dad! Oh my god!" He laughs and ruffles my hair.

I've watched *Morning Live Kidz!* my whole life. Me and Chloe scream at the Slime Game every single Saturday. I want to go and wake her up to tell her. I can't believe they've seen the video and want me to go on the show. It's all happening. Leo Leggett has made it all happen. I want to call him and say thank you, but Dad says it can wait until the morning.

Just as I'm imagining me and Leo sitting on the *Morning Live Kidz!* sofa together, chatting to the hosts, a picture of Skyla crying on the bench flashes through my brain. How can this all be happening to me when she's in so much trouble? I have to figure out a plan to help her. As soon as I have said yes to this email!

CHAPTER 19

Apparently Iron Man did a tuxedo range.

It wasn't his strong suit.

A tuxedo arrives the next morning. It fits perfectly.
I'm not sure how they know my size. It is starting to
feel like the whole world knows an awful lot about
me. The suit makes me feel like a tiny grown-up. Like
it's a costume and I need to be a different person when
I'm wearing it. I practise some faces in the mirror.
Laughing elegantly at a joke and listening gravely to
someone.

To be honest, I would rather wear my trainers and
hoodie, but I think it would be a bit rude, seeing as
the Leo Leggett team sent it over specially.

Mum and Dad have had a long chat with Sal about

what time I'm going to be back and who is going to be looking after me and loads of other stuff. When I walk into the living room in the tuxedo, Mum immediately bursts into tears.

"Mum, you really have to stop crying."

"But look at you and—"

"I know, it's the baby," I say, rolling my eyes.

"No, it's not the baby – it's you and your gorgeous face." Then she sniffs and wipes her eyes. "I'm not sure I want the rest of the world to have you. I want to keep you for a while longer before you become a global superstar."

"Too late, lady, have you seen T-T-TikTok?! I have fans in Japan. I'm everywhere." I let her ruffle my hair. Secretly I quite like that it's me that has made her cry for once, rather than some cheesy advert or because she dropped a saucepan or something.

The car they send to pick me up is super fancy and there are loads of buttons in the back that change all the lighting. I keep changing the colour and opening and closing the windows until the driver says that I am going to make him crash. So then I take loads of pictures of me posing and WhatsApp them to The Regulars.

But no one sees it so I just end up scrolling through Twitter and YouTube comments again, some nice ones and some mean ones, which I try to ignore. The Regulars will all be on their holidays. Splashing in pools and sleeping in tents. For a moment I feel envious of their normal lives; if it weren't for the baby coming then we would probably be in a campsite in France too. Then I shake my head and laugh to myself, remembering where I am. I'm famous. There's nothing better than that, right?

Sal said that she'll be waiting for me when I get to the venue. As the car eventually pulls in outside a big hotel, there are huge groups of people all dressed up standing in the street and I wonder if Sal will find me in the crowd. There are people in gold dresses, with birds in their hair and high shoes. There are men in huge skirts and there is a woman in an orange suit on stilts. Behind some barriers are crowds of normal people desperately trying to get a glimpse of the rich and famous.

Photographers snap away at some of the most dramatic-looking people, getting right in their faces and shouting questions. It looks exciting and scary and wonderful and horrible all at the same time. I stand next to the driver and scan the crowd, searching for Leo, and then Sal breaks away from a group of people and comes towards me with a smile.

"You made it! Follow me. Leo is on the red carpet waiting for you."

Leo Leggett is on the red carpet, waiting for *me* – this definitely beats a rainy campsite! I follow her through the skirts and sequins and inside the building. We come to a red carpet with a huge light-up sign saying "THE BRITISH COMEDY AWARDS". There are comedians being photographed who I recognize from panel shows on the telly. They all look so shiny. The photographers here are dressed in fancy suits too and don't get in people's faces like the ones outside do.

I see Leo before he sees me, and I think he looks a bit bored and fed up, staring at his phone. He's wearing a tuxedo exactly like mine. When he sees me, his face changes into a big smile, and he puts his phone away.

"Billy! My man! Finally! Let's get these pictures taken, shall we? Look at us – we scrub up all right, don't we?"

A man with a microphone rushes over. "Who is this, Leo?"

"This is the fabulous Billy Plimpton. He's a young comic with a stammer who I have taken under my wing as part of my anti-bullying campaign. Watch out for him; he is going to become even more famous than me!" Then he winks into the camera, leans towards it and says, "Say no to bullying, folks." The man looks at me and smiles, about to open his mouth, but Leo puts his arm on my shoulder and steers me away, saying, "You've got to be careful with journalists, Billy. They will take you down any chance they get."

Then he leads me in front of the light-up sign on the red carpet. The cameras start flashing and Leo pulls funny faces and points at me and asks me to point at him. Then we stand back to back and fold our arms, looking at each other over our shoulders. It feels like we are a real double act.

But someone comes and leads Leo off, and I'm left on the red carpet. When a very tall woman with blue hair stands next to me, the photographers all tell me to move along. I try to follow Leo into the crowd but can't keep up, and for a second I panic that I won't find him again and will be lost in a sea of famous people all night. Then Sal sweeps in next to me, links my arm and takes me through the crowd towards our table.

The room is huge and there must be hundreds of tables all with candles and chandeliers above them. A lady with bright red glittery lipstick gives us a bag full of free stuff as we walk past. I start rummaging through it – there are pens, books, a T-shirt and a watch! Sal laughs as I am pulling things out and showing her. She says I can have a proper look through when we get to our table.

The massive room looks twinkly and fancy. We are on table 71. I make sure I remember where it is located, in case I need a wee and get lost on the way back. I'm good at remembering where things are. Mum always makes me remember where we park in big multi-storey car parks or else she'll get lost and end up wandering around pressing the unlock button on the car keys, hoping to see the flash of lights.

I'm sitting next to some people I don't recognize. They are old and look important in a rich kind of way, what my dad calls "the money men". I was hoping that I would be sat with a load of famous people, but none of them are familiar. On a table next to us I see a lady from one of my favourite panel shows, and when she catches me staring at her she smiles and waves. I go red and look away.

Leo is sitting on the other side of our huge table,

looking down at his phone again, too far away to talk to. I really want to talk to him about *Morning Live Kidz!* and what we are going to do on it; surely we need to rehearse? It'll have to wait until after dinner, I guess. It would have been cool if we were sitting next to each other, then we could have talked about our routine and he could introduce me to everyone. I wonder if I could swap with the lady next to him, but as I am about to get up and ask, the food arrives.

The meal is brought to the tables by a stream of waiters in black and white. I hear one person saying that the Queen used to ice-skate in this room, but I don't think that can be true as there is no ice – it's not even cold, it's roasting. Anyway, I don't think the Queen would have ice-skated – it's not very regal, is it?

After we've eaten three courses of food with dots of red on the plates and foams and sprinkles and crisps made out of cheese, someone comes on to the stage and starts announcing the awards.

At first, it's exciting seeing people I recognize from the telly crying while they give a speech and others pulling funny faces and making jokes. It's especially exciting when the lady from the panel show on the next table wins. The whole table erupts into screams and shouts and I clap extra loud as if I know her too, and they all stand up and hug a lot. Maybe I need to add that to my list of when to hug:

- When you win a massive award – hug *everyone*.

"And now the award for best comedy newcomer. Take note, people, this young man could be the next big thing." I look up at the stage and imagine that it's my name they're about to call. I start imagining what I would say and who I would thank. What joke would I tell? My fantasy is interrupted:

"The award goes to Kit Parsons."

Everyone claps and cheers and a comedian gets on the stage to accept the award. He looks really young, not much older than me. He giggles and holds up the trophy and does a funny little dance.

Out of the corner of my eye I notice Leo get up and hurry round the table to Sal. He starts whispering into her ear. I can tell that something's wrong, but I pretend to keep watching the speech. Leo gets up and walks out of the huge room, weaving through the tables, and I look back to the comic finishing his speech.

"Finally, massive thanks to all of the comedy legends who have supported me when I have been terrified at gigs and helped me to get through some tough moments – you know who you are." Then Kit pauses. "To anyone who has *not* supported me, who stole my jokes or put me down or said that I would not make it – you also know who you are. WATCH YOUR BACK!"

The audience do a huge "Oooooh" as he says the last words, and then everyone laughs at themselves, as though they are being childish. I'm sure he is looking over at our table, and when he sees the empty seat where Leo was he smiles.

Leo doesn't come back.

The ceremony seems to go on for ever and by midnight when they are still giving out award after award, I think the whole royal family could ice-skate on to the stage and I wouldn't have the energy to clap or cheer. I slowly sink lower into my chair and, just as they announce the award for Best Live Comedy Production, I feel my eyelids closing.

Half an hour later I wake up to Sal gently shaking me in my seat. "Let's get you to your car, Billy."

"But I haven't talked to Leo," I mumble. "We need to plan *Morning Live Kidz!*"

"He's already gone. Don't worry about that. He'll be in touch."

CHAPTER 20

What do you call an English teacher who is addicted to social media?

An insta-grammar.

The next day, as I'm walking to Mrs Gibbens's, holding a huge box of chocolates that were delivered to me this morning from "Leo's team" under one arm and Scraggles's lead in the other, I hear my name being called.

"B-B-Billy Plimpton!"

This is a thing now, people shouting at me in the street. I keep walking. It's nice that they recognize me but hearing my name being called like that, with a stammer, kind of reminds me of when Blakemore used to do it at school. I wish the clip that Leo had put up hadn't included the stammer, but I guess maybe then none of this would be happening, would it? Maybe without my stammer I would be a nobody. The thought makes me shudder. I want to become Billy Plimpton – the Funniest Boy in the World, not B-B-Billy Plimpton – the Funny Kid with the Stammer.

The original video that Leo uploaded has been watched over two million times. I'm not quite sure how it's got so big; the actual clip only shows me walking on to the stage and saying my name. I don't even tell a joke. All the comments underneath talk about my stammer.

OMG he is SOOOOO cute. 😍😍😍

Proud stammerer here too. 👏

Go, Team Billy.

#Stammeringcomedian

Mostly the comments are really lovely, but there are a few that are mean:

That kid is so annoying.

Not even remotely funny. 👎

I bet he doesn't even have a stutter #fakestutter

Even though there are way more of the nice comments, it's the bad ones I keep thinking about and go back to and read again and again. It's weird how that happens – if a teacher tells me ten nice things and then says one bad thing, I always remember the bad one. I'm not sure if that happens to everyone, if it's just the way human beings are, but it's a bit annoying. I would much rather be focusing on the good stuff. I can't help myself, though.

The one comment I read over and over more than any of the others is Leo's comment underneath the original post.

A star is born? I'd better watch my back, eh?

The pictures from the awards were all online this morning. Me and Leo in our tuxedos, shining out from every corner of the internet. Comments about how cute we look build up underneath the picture. In the pictures we look so happy, like we're best friends, mucking about and making each other laugh. I wish that was true. I wish he had spoken to me after the photos and we had made each other laugh until we cried, like me and The Regulars do. I wish the way we look in the picture was real, but it was not like that at all. I guess there is still time to become like the photos, to make him laugh and to get to know him better. I am going on *Morning Live Kidz!* with him next Saturday. Maybe that's when it will start feeling real. When I get to Mrs Gibbens's, she's got a jigsaw out on the table.

"It's a woodland scene, Billy. The nurses thought it was a good idea. A bit boring, if you ask me. Will you do some while me and Scraggles have a snuggle? I can tell them I did it, then."

At first, I'm quite into sorting the edges from the middle pieces. There is something so boring about it that it's almost relaxing but, as I'm finding edges with hedgehogs and badgers on them, I check my phone. Nothing from Skyla. I've been texting her loads, but she's vanished again. I know I need to come up with a plan to help her. I just don't know how.

A notification from TikTok pops up on the screen and then it's too late: I drift away from the woodland creatures and thinking about how to help Skyla, into the land of likes. Scrolling through photos from last night. Even when there is nothing new to check, I keep moving from one platform to the other, just in case something happens.

Mum is worried about how much time I'm spending on my phone. She says that I have become obsessed, but I think she would be pretty obsessed too if she'd become an overnight sensation.

On my way back down the street later, after Scraggles has eaten an entire packet of ham and Mrs Gibbens has drifted off to sleep, I hear my name again.

"Billy!" I try to ignore it. But I hear it again and then again. This must be a super fan! I turn around and see Mr Osho jogging down the street behind me.

"Oh, sorry, sir. I didn't know it was you!"

"Just thought it was one of your many fans, eh?"

"Kind of." I shrug. He bends over and strokes Scraggles.

"I'll walk with you, Billy. I saw you and wanted to check in, see how you are doing since the festival."

I tell him about the British Comedy Awards and how exciting it all was. I don't tell him about how I can't seem to stop checking for negative comments or that I didn't even really get to talk to Leo. In fact, he pretty much blanked me after the photos on the red carpet.

Mr Osho listens and then he says, "And what about Skyla? How's she doing?"

I stop and look at him. It's like he knows. He can't, though, and Skyla's told me not to say anything. I don't know what to do so I shrug and ask him what he means.

"She had a bit of time off school and I couldn't get through to her mum before the holidays, so I just wondered how she was doing, that's all."

"She's f-f-fine," I say, and we walk on together. Then I add, "She'll be fine. Skyla's really tough."

"Yup, she's tough, all right." Mr Osho smiles. "Sometimes people are tough, though, because they have to be. It doesn't mean they don't need looking after too. You know you can tell me if you think she needs help. Just because it's the holidays doesn't mean I'm not your teacher, right? I'm still here for you."

"Yeah," I say. I think back to how Mr Osho has helped me. How kind he has been and how he never told me what to do; how he just listened. Maybe bumping into him today is a sign that I need to tell him. I think about how angry Skyla would be, though, and how I told her I wouldn't tell anyone. So I decide to be clever about it.

"Sir, can I ask you a qu-qu-question?" I ask as we stop to let Scraggles wee on a lamp post.

"Of course."

"It's a hypothetical question."

"I'm glad to hear that you are still using such good vocabulary even in the summer holidays, Billy. I love a hypothetical question, so hit me with it."

"If s-s-someone's mum w-w-was drinking loads – and I mean LOADS – what would happen to them? Hypothetically."

He thinks about this, looking a bit worried. I can feel myself go red as I know that I have not done a very good job of covering up the truth.

"Well," he says, "hypothetically speaking, if the parent was unable to care properly for the child, then the social services would offer some help or support."

"L-Like what?" I ask.

"It would depend on the circumstances, Billy. I need a little more 'hypothetical' detail. What exactly is happening in this imaginary family? Is there violence or neglect?"

"Well, there is shouting and vomit – hypothetical vomit, of course," I add quickly.

"I think it would definitely be something that social services would want to look into. It might be that the hypothetical person could be supported in the home, with getting off the booze and getting some extra childcare. Or in extreme circumstances it might be that the child needed to be looked after elsewhere until the parent got back on their feet. But without any details I couldn't really say. What I do know is that a good friend would hypothetically be doing the right thing to find help and ask for support." He smiles at me and all of a sudden I feel like I might have made a huge mistake. What if he goes and tells on Skyla's mum? Skyla would never talk to me again.

I'm so worried about that, I barely notice Mr Osho saying goodbye. When he's gone, I try to call Skyla. I hear the calling tone ring out over and over and I keep trying until she eventually picks up.

"Skyla, I think I might have done something terrible," I blurt out.

"Billy, I can't talk now," she whispers. It sounds echoey and there are different noises in the background.

"I think I accidentally told Mr Osho about your mum," I say. "I'm sorry. I'm just so worried about you."

"It doesn't matter, Billy."

"What? I thought you would be so cross." Then

I hear a beeping sound and people's voices. "Where are you, Skyla?"

"I'm at the hospital," she says. "It got really bad last night." She pauses and I wonder if she is still there, and then her voice comes back sounding muffled and scared, "She wouldn't wake up. I thought she was going to die." Then I hear someone saying her name in the background. "I've got to go, Billy." She hangs up.

CHAPTER 21

What do books wear on stormy days?

Rain quotes.

It rains for the next two days. Not like summer rain, like relentless, torrential rain. It feels like the world is ending. There are pictures of floods on the news and people sitting on the roofs of their houses.

I've been calling Skyla non-stop. I'm keeping count now and I have tried calling her fifty-two times, left twelve messages and texted her fifteen times. She hasn't responded. Now I'm even more addicted to checking my phone than I was before. I keep thinking about the sound of her voice and the beeps of the hospital in the background. Is her mum OK? Is Skyla OK? What was happening? I try to remember her exact words. *"She wouldn't wake up. I thought she was going to die."* How can drinking wine make you die, though? None of it makes sense.

When I can't stand not knowing what's happening to her any more, I walk in the rain over to her house and bang on the door. I'm calling her name, but I know that no one is behind the darkened windows.

"SKYLA!" I try for the fifth time.

A neighbour pokes their head out from the house next door. "They got picked up in an ambulance the other night, not been back since."

I stop banging. *Where are you, Skyla?* My phone beeps a message sound, as if in response to my thoughts.

At a foster house.

I start walking and quickly tap in a message asking where. My phone beeps again.

Downham Road. Theres a bench
opposite the chippy.

I start running and tap in a response.

I'm coming.

I jump on a bus down the main road and keep track of where I am going on Google maps. I watch the little dot moving towards Downham Road. Why has Skyla been sent so far away? I don't even really know what a foster house is. Is it with loads of kids, like a school that you sleep at, or is it just a normal house? Will Skyla live at Downham Road for ever now? It's hard to keep focused on the little moving dot as my brain floods with questions and worries. When I look down and see the dot move past where I'm heading, I ring the bell and jump off.

I'm glad that Mum taught me how to use buses. When she first got pregnant, before the baby took over her whole body and mind, she set me a challenge.

"Right, Billy, I'm not being your taxi service for the rest of your life, so you need to learn how to get yourself around." She handed me a bus pass and a timetable and then told me that I had two hours to get to Abbeycliffe Road, which is two different buses away, take a picture of myself outside the deli to prove that I got there and then come home via the ice rink and the football ground. She wanted pictures at all of them and then at the last minute added an extra stop.

...nd rubbed her tummy. I wasn't too happy about being sent all over town and I missed my stop three times and had to run back on myself, but when I got home and showed her all of the selfies and delivered the pastry she was really pleased with me and said, "That's your pastry, by the way."

"I thought it was for the baby?"

"It is. You will always be my baby too, Billy, even though you're big enough to travel on buses all over town!"

I like timetables and maps and figuring out the best routes to places so it's no problem finding the chippy and the bench on Downham Road.

As I'm walking towards it, I can see her through the rain. She's sitting on the bench, head held high and proud. Not at all diminished by the rain. A lorry drives past me and water splashes up from its wheels. As it approaches Skyla's bench I see a huge puddle on the road next to her. I call out to warn her, but it's too late. The lorry hits the floodwater and a wave sweeps over Skyla and the bench. She just sits there upright, not moving.

"I'm already drenched," she says, not looking at me. Another car heads our way and I hide behind the bench when the water swooshes up from the tyres.

"It's actually OK when you just give in to it, Billy. Sit down. It's like being in the sea."

"Are you OK, Skyla? What's g-going on?"

"Sit down and I'll tell you."

"You are completely bonkers!" I shout as she gets covered again. She just laughs and waits for me to join her.

Eventually I give in and go and sit and wait for the next car to cover us in water. The cold and shock of it make me gasp.

"Once me and Mum were walking to school when I was little. We were running up the road trying to dodge the splashes from the cars. It was so much fun. When we mistimed a run and a car soaked us we both screamed and then laughed. Then the game changed. We were running to *try* and get the cars to splash us. It was one of the best days ever." She looks sad and happy at the same

CHAPTER 22

I told a joke on my Zoom meeting.

It wasn't even remotely funny.

On Friday, I get an email.

> Leo is so glad that you will be joining him on
> *Morning Live Kidz!* He has space for a quick
> Zoom this afternoon to prep for the show.
> Invite attached.

"Hey, Billy boy! How you doing?!"

Leo is sitting by a swimming pool somewhere hot. I'm not sure how on earth he will get back in time to get to the show tomorrow, but before I get a chance to ask, he carries on.

"So, Billy, our first outing as a double act, eh? I can't wait. I've done the show loads, they all love me there. So, just follow my lead and everything will be great."

"Wh-Wh-Wh-What will we talk about, though? D-D-D-Do I need to t-t-t-tell any jokes or stories or anything?"

"No, kid, honestly, leave it to me. You're awesome, you know that – but I know how to handle this sort of thing."

A waitress comes on to the screen and brings him a fancy-looking drink and he winks at her, takes a sip and then looks back at me.

"Now, Billy, I wanted to give you a heads up about something – no biggie, but it's worth you knowing. The newspapers have it in for me right now – which is even more reason for us to go out there and smash it. But you might hear some nonsense about me. Don't listen to it, Billy. Just rumours and gossip from comedians who never made it. It's just part of the job, I'm afraid. Everyone is jealous, that's all. But if they come asking you questions, you tell them to get lost."

He looks relaxed on his sun lounger, but I can tell that he is not as chilled as he appears. His eyes nervously flick around every now and then and he looks tired and anxious. I feel a bit sorry for him. It must be horrible having people make up lies about you.

"OK," I say. "And if anyone asks me anything I'll say you're really nice and kind."

"Attaboy. Oh, and one more thing. Tomorrow, if you meet that terrible comic Kit Parsons, run!"

I remember Kit Parsons from the comedy awards. "W-W-Why?" I ask.

Leo gives me a serious look. "He's trouble. I would be scared of running into him on a dark night, that's for sure. He went for me once – punched me for no reason. Stay well away, OK?"

"OK," I say, feeling a bit nervous. I didn't realize comics went around punching people.

"And if any journalist or comic ever asks you anything about me, just tell them I'm your hero, OK?"

"Y-Y-You *are* my hero," I say. And I mean it.

"Thanks, Billy. It was great timing, finding you." I'm not sure what he is talking about. Great timing for what? "Anyway, I'll see you at the show. So long, buddy."

Then the screen goes blank, and I'm left shaking my head. Something feels funny – and not in a good way. But I squish the feeling down. I am about to go on my favourite TV show with a famous comedian. What could be better?

I get loads of messages from The Regulars and Skyla and everyone wishing me luck for tomorrow. Literally EVERYONE will be watching. Not knowing what I'm going to say or do is terrifying, but I can trust Leo, can't I? I mean, he is the best comedian in the world; he knows exactly how to make people laugh, so I just need to do what he says. I'll let him take the lead and go along with it. And I'll have some of my joke book jokes ready in my head, just in case.

A huge parcel arrives later that afternoon with my name on it. When I open it, I see loads of branded clothes and trainers. I have no idea where they have come from; they must have cost a fortune. When I find a card at the bottom of the box, it reads: *A gift from us all at the JD Group. Feel free to wear during your upcoming events with Leo Leggett – he's welcome to tag us on his socials!*

They are giving me stuff for free! I can't believe it. This must be what happens when you get famous! I decide what to wear for *Morning Live Kidz!* and lay it all out in my bedroom. I keep looking at the trainers as I go to sleep.

When my alarm goes off in the morning, I feel so

excited that I get pins and needles all over my body. I have to stomp around my bedroom to get rid of them, but Mum shouts and tells me to stop making such a racket.

The TV people offered us a car, but Dad said he would drive. I would rather have got the TV car – it wouldn't have banana skins in the back pockets and smell of sprouts.

When we get out of the car and walk into the studio I see lots of photographers hanging around outside. I wonder if they are waiting for Leo – or me. I smile and wave on my way into the studio, flashes of bulbs lighting up my face. My famous face!

CHAPTER 23

What do hedgehogs eat?

Prickled onions.

"Hello, good morning, huzzah, whoop whoop, wakey wakey! IT'S *MORNING LIVE KIDZ!*"

Someone at the front holds up a sign saying: *Cheer* and the studio audience go wild, clapping and whooping. I'm standing at the side, clutching my bottle of shells in my pocket, with Melanie, who is looking after me. She's nice. She has really curly hair and only looks a few years older than me. She showed me to my dressing room, which has my name on the door! It also has loads of juice and pop in a tiny fridge and a TV on the wall. There was another goody bag full of free stuff too! Chocolate, some mini cakes, a key ring and a phone case. Famous people don't need to buy anything!

I've been here since six a.m. Dad and Chloe are in the audience. I thought Chloe was going to explode with excitement. I don't think she actually went to sleep last night.

A hair and make-up lady sat me in front of a mirror and brushed different powders on to my face with a soft brush – it was weird, she was so close that I could feel her breath on my cheek. It was a bit awkward, but the brush was soft and it felt lovely and I almost didn't want her to stop. Then she combed my hair and said that I was "ready to go".

After that Melanie took me to a canteen and got me some breakfast and told me what was going to happen.

"You're on at eight thirty. They're doing a comedy segment and will be talking to you and Leo first, then Kit Parsons. Do you know Kit?"

"Yeah, I mean, no, I don't know him, but I've seen him."

Melanie looked around, leaned in and whispered, "He used to work with Leo too, but let's just say they don't speak any more."

"They w-w-worked together? Why d-don't they like each other?" I whispered back.

She shrugged. "You would have to ask Leo."

I remembered seeing Kit up on the stage at the comedy awards. His pointed words as he looked at Leo's empty chair. I remembered Leo warning me off Kit, saying he could be violent.

Now we are standing in the wings, waiting.

"Is Leo here yet?" I whisper.

"No. He will turn up seconds before we record – he always does." The way she says it makes it sound as though she doesn't think much of him. It surprises me as I've only ever heard people going on about how much they love him and how funny he is. Now it seems that there are people who don't like him at all.

"He must be really busy, I guess," I say, trying to stick up for him. After all, he's the only reason that I'm here. Melanie smiles and looks like she feels sorry for me or something. It feel like there are little warning bells going off in my brain, but I have no idea what they are warning me of. I start taking deep breaths to calm myself down. Maybe it's just nerves. It's normal to be nervous; I'm about to go on the telly in front of millions of people. I might not be able to even speak. Thinking about my stammer just makes everything worse and so I grab my shells and imagine Granny Bread tipping her head back and laughing at one of my jokes. Just as I'm starting to enjoy the image Melanie interrupts it.

"So, they will bring you on first, just sit on the couch. Mitch and Jaya will ask you some questions and have the usual chat then Leo will join you. You've seen the show before, haven't you?"

I nod.

"They are really nice. You'll have loads of fun."

"D-d-d-do they know that I stammer?"

"Absolutely. If they interrupt you then it's only because it's live and they have to get to the break on time." This worries me a bit – if I have to talk fast with a stammer, it could end badly. My worry must show on my face because Melanie smiles and says, "Don't worry, you'll be great. It's time."

We are just waiting for them to call my name and I will walk out in front of the cameras, which are swooping around all over the place, the audience who seem to clap and whoop whenever the sign is held up and Jaya and Mitch, the hosts who I've watched on my telly every Saturday since I can remember.

Then, as I am running through my latest favourite joke in my head, I feel Melanie tapping me and gently pushing me forward.

"You're on!" she whispers.

As I step out to the sound of clapping, I see Jaya and Mitch standing by the sofa and dancing to the welcome music, but Leo is nowhere to be seen. I can't do this on my own.

"Billy Plimpton!" Jaya says, giving me a high five. She's grinning and relaxed, which immediately calms me down a bit.

We sit down and I get comfy on the sofa. "So, how does it feel to be an internet sensation and the youngest new comic taking the world by storm?" Mitch says.

"Ah, you know, it's j-j-j-just another d-d-d-d-day at the office." I shrug. They both laugh and then turn to the cameras, telling my story and explaining who I am. It feels weird having them talk about me while I'm sitting there. I have no idea what to do with my face. I don't even know if the cameras are pointing at me and so I start pulling really serious listening faces as they talk. Nodding my head and stroking my chin. The audience start laughing, even though there is no sign telling them to. I like the sound of the laughter and so make my face even more serious. They laugh even more. It's weird, I'm barely doing anything. Maybe now that I'm famous people will just laugh no matter what I do. Then they introduce Leo.

"Now that we've met Billy, it's time to introduce the man who discovered him. The biggest comedian of all time. The man who knows all the stars, who has won all of the awards and who has had the fastest-selling comedy tour ever recorded. Raise the roof, everyone, it's only LEO LEGGETT!!!!" The audience go wild and start screaming and stamping their feet as Leo walks out on to the stage, beaming and waving. When he gets to the sofa, he gestures for me to stand up and when I do, he picks me up, lifts me above his head and holds me up like a prize. The audience are laughing, but I don't really like the feeling of it. When he puts me down he shakes my hand really hard so that my whole body wobbles. Then he gives me a little wink and whispers, "Don't mess this up, kid." He is smiling as he says it, but suddenly I feel utterly terrified.

"OK, before we get to talk to you guys, it's quickfire questions time, and you know who asks the questions on this show."

The whole audience start shouting, "PODGE HEG! PODGE HEG! PODGE HEG!" and Podge Heg the angry hedgehog puppet in a waistcoat pops up behind the sofa.

I didn't know that I was doing quickfire questions with Podge Heg; this is like every single anxiety dream I have ever had rolled into one. This is bad. Fast questions asked by an angry puppet, with no time to think of a good answer AND it's all going out live on the telly.

"Peas or carrots?" Podge Heg shouts at Leo in his rough, shrill voice.

"Carrots," Leo says, pointing to a gold chain around his neck and then doing a kind of R&B dance move while licking his necklace.

The audience laugh, then Podge Heg looks at me.

"P-P-P-P-P…" I know that I'm never going to get the word out, let alone think of a joke to go with it. Podge Heg doesn't wait to find out.

"Lions or tigers?"

"Hedgehogs?" Leo answers coyly and winks and blows a kiss at Podge Heg, who pretends to faint and fall off the back of the sofa. I know if I was watching at home like I normally do I would be laughing at this. Even though Podge Heg is a bit babyish he's still pretty funny, and Leo knows exactly what he's doing, he's so quick. I manage to get through the quickfire questions without saying a word. When Podge Heg disappears Mitch and Jaya sit back down.

"So, Leo," says Jaya, "how on earth did you find Billy?"

"How did I find him? I was looking for a pound for the bus and there he was in my pocket next to my chewing gum." The audience howl at this, but I'm not sure why. It's not that funny.

"Billy, how does it feel to be sitting next to the most famous comedian in the world?"

"Careful how you answer this one, Billy, I'm bigger than you, remember."

"Yeah, but I can tell my mum on you, and she's hormonal," I say, quick as a flash, with no hint of a stammer. The audience laugh hard, and it feels so good. It may be the only thing that I have managed to say, but at least it made them laugh. I start to think that this double-act thing could actually work, but when I turn back to Leo, I see something flash across his face – anger. It's gone in a second and only I notice it.

"T-T-Tell everyone, Billy. How exactly I discovered you." Did he just stammer? I'm not sure if I heard it right. Maybe he just got a bit stuck like everyone does, but something about it felt different. I look back to Jaya and Mitch and they are waiting for me to speak.

"It was at Field Fest," I say, trying to smile. "I d-d-d-did a g-g-g-g-g-g-gig."

"He did do a g-g-g-g-g-g-g-gig," Leo says, grinning,

and the whole audience laugh. Then he pinches me on the cheek and winks at me again. He just copied my stammer. In front of millions of people on TV. He copied my stammer and everyone is laughing. Even Jaya and Mitch are laughing.

"It was a pretty terrible g-g-g-g-gig, wasn't it, Billy?" He doesn't wait for me to answer. "Full of awful dad jokes. But I saw something in little Billy here. Star potential, so I reached out to him. We've had some great fun since then, writing together, working on material. He's a good sport. I think you might be seeing a bit more of us as a double act. What do you say, Billy?" Then, before I can answer, he reaches out to me and grabs the back of my head, nods it up and down forcefully and starts speaking with his mouth closed as though I am his ventriloquist's dummy. He gives me a silly, high-pitched voice: "Yes, everyone, you will be seeing loads more of me and my uncle Leo."

I want to tell him to stop, but the words won't come. I start to panic. My mouth can't even begin to make a sound.

Then he turns my head sharply towards his. "See, it's easy, Billy, you can talk like a real boy."

I hear the laughter of the audience and I can feel

my throat getting tight and my eyes are getting wet. Then he pretends to be me again, "Oh, thanks, Uncle Leo, thanks so much for making me a superstar."

The audience are all laughing so hard. My face is going bright red. This is horrible. It's worse than when I got stuck reading in front of the class or when I was in my French oral exam. It's worse than anything Blakemore ever did. As all of these memories are flying through my brain, I can hear Leo chatting easily with the hosts. Then they thank us for our time, and he says, "Well, that's it from us." He nods my head again, speaking for me. "Are we going home, Uncle Leo?"

"Yes, Billy, time to go home and get back in your box." Then he lifts me up off the sofa and flings me over his shoulder. That's when the tear falls from my eye, and I see it hitting the stage.

CHAPTER 24

**What did the banana say to the banana
bully?**

You hurt my peelings.

When Leo carries me off the stage and puts me down, I
feel dizzy like I might collapse. He slaps me on the back
and says, "Great stuff, Billy. Really great. I'll be in touch,
yeah?" I wipe my eyes and watch him stride away.

It's all a complete blur. I'm not sure what just
happened. I look back on to the stage and see Jaya and
Mitch talking to Kit Parsons. No one else seemed to
think anything was wrong.

"You were great!" Melanie smiles.

She says I was great and so did Leo. So maybe it
was. But then why do I feel so bad?

"B-B-But…" I can't get any words out as they are so muddled in my brain. I don't even know what I want to say. I'm so confused.

"Everyone was laughing so much. Look, they put this clip out on the socials and people are loving you already."

She shows me her phone and I see Leo moving my head up and down on the sofa. The likes are ticking up. I feel the tears pricking my eyes again.

"N-N-No, that's n-n-n-n-n-n-n—"

"I'll take you to your dressing room and you can chill out for a bit."

In the dressing room my mind is whirring. I stare at myself in the mirror, questions forming in my head.

"How could people not see?" I whisper. "He was bullying me, wasn't he?" So why didn't I say something, or do something? Why did I just let it happen? I wipe my eyes and wash my face in the little sink.

I can't figure out how I should be feeling. I wanted people to laugh at me – and they did laugh. I should be happy – but I'm not. I feel my phone vibrating and can't bring myself to look at it. It's probably Dad and Chloe. Did they think it was funny, like the rest of the world? I can't face talking to anyone. Not if I have to smile and nod and pretend that I enjoyed being manhandled and mimicked. I don't want to be in a double act if that's what I have to do – even if it is with Leo Leggett.

There is a knock at the door, and I quickly wipe my eyes and open it thinking that it'll be Melanie again, but Kit Parsons is standing there, leaning against the door frame, his hair flopping into his eyes.

"Hey, man, I saw your segment with Leo."

I feel so embarrassed; I'm pretty sure that my face is still red from crying. I wipe my eyes again and look up at his kind-looking face and instantly remember Leo's words.

"I would be scared of running into him on a dark night, that's for sure."

Kit doesn't look violent as he leans on the door smiling, but that somehow makes him even scarier.

"I just wanted to say hello away from the madness. Check you're OK."

"Y-Yeah," I whisper.

"Did you enjoy that?" he asks, smiling.

I shrug and sigh. I don't want to say anything else, in case he loved it and found it as funny as everyone else seemed to. Or in case he is as terrifying as Leo said. I don't want to get punched.

"Ha, I know the feeling. It's surreal. Especially

when it's live, it feels like a runaway train. You did great, man, to just get through it and not make a run for it. That's what I wanted to do the first time I did live telly ... and I wasn't doing it next to Leo Leggett." The way he says Leo's name makes me think that he *knows* that something is not right.

What happened between him and Leo? I need to find out. I try to ignore Leo's words about Kit ringing around in my head. I look again at his kind face and decide to trust my instinct. I manage to whisper my words.

"Th-thanks. I don't think Leo w-w-w-would have let me run away even if I'd tried! D-D-D-Do you want to come in and have some juice? I've g-g-got a little f-f-fridge full of it. I'm not sure how much juice they thought a t-t-t-twelve-year-old could drink, but I need help."

"Sure, let's have a drinking competition," he says, stepping through the door.

Kit sits down and asks me what got me into comedy. It turns out that he's only seventeen himself and he started two years ago so he's kind of a kid too, but he seems so confident, like he knows exactly what he's doing. When I tell him about meeting Leo at the festival and him posting me online his face changes.

"Look, I know it's exciting when a big name like Leo pays you attention," he says, finishing his second carton of juice. "But be careful there."

"W-W-What do you mean?"

"I'm not one to bad-mouth other comics, but … well … Leo might be the face of that anti-bullying campaign, but believe me he is not a good guy. I've been there myself. All Leo cares about is himself. Be careful."

"I think it's t-t-too l-late," I mumble.

Then it all comes out. That none of what just happened onstage was planned. That I didn't like being picked up and mimicked. That Leo Leggett made fun of my stammer on live TV in front of the world and the world seemed to think it was hilarious.

When I tell Kit all about Leo stealing the "It's the baby" line after the meeting at his house, Kit puts his head in his hands.

"He's such a…" And then before he uses a swear word, he squashes his empty carton in his fist.

"You're a kid, for god's sake. Who nicks jokes off a kid and then humiliates them like that?"

"I know, but he made me famous, didn't he?"

"I hope you didn't give him any more material?"

"I don't think so." I hesitate, then ask, "Has he done this before?"

Kit takes a deep breath. "He nicks jokes all the time, mate. He takes new comedians under his wing and then steals their fresh material. He did it to me."

"What?"

"Oh yeah. I was his protégé, didn't you know? He sent me chocolates and video games."

"He sent me a pyramid of brownies."

"That's what he does. Makes you feel special and then destroys your confidence. Tells you you're great but then says you have no jokes worth telling. When you went to his house did you meet Wayne? The dog he does all his material about?"

"No..." I say.

"That's because Wayne is *my* dog! All the dog stuff was mine."

"N-No way?!"

"I told you, he's done it loads. He told me it was normal to share material, but it always seemed to go one way. Eventually I told him I'd had enough. I thought that was the end of it, but the next time we were on a panel show together, he humiliated me. Made fun of me. Stole my punchlines. Made *me* the joke. The audience were laughing at me, not with me.

I was a mess afterwards – thought about giving up comedy for a while. Glad I stuck at it, though." He shook his head. "Most comics hate him. I honestly don't think he's got an original joke."

"He told me that was *my* problem. That I needed to ditch the joke book jokes and write my own stuff."

"Yeah, and he's not wrong, but you don't do it by nicking other people's ideas or belittling them onstage, do you?"

"No," I say. "He told me to be careful of you."

"Ha! I bet he did. He wouldn't want me warning you about him, would he?"

"He s-s-said you had a h-h-history of violence."

"What?!"

"Did you punch Leo?"

"I threw a whoopee cushion at him when I found out he had stolen my jokes! You should have seen him: he was nearly crying, threatening to call the police. So yes, I am guilty of whoopee-cushion violence, Billy, I hold my hands up."

I smile. I like Kit. I feel like he is real. So much recently has not felt real, but he seems normal and honest and how I thought it would be to talk to a real comedian. Why didn't I figure this out sooner? I should have known at Leo's house or at the awards.

Thinking about it all now, it was obvious from the beginning that he was a horrible person. I just drowned out any warnings and told myself what I wanted to believe.

"I w-w-wish there was something we could do to stop him."

"Me too, mate. Believe me I have tried, but audiences don't care; they love him too much. The papers were about to run a piece on him; we got all excited that the story was going to break – and then he did the whole anti-bullying thing and your double act started up and his people managed to bury it. One day he will get what's coming to him."

"I h-h-have to do something," I say.

Kit sighs. "Let me know if you have any bright ideas. It would have to be pretty big, though. No one will listen or care unless it is impossible not to. I would totally back you up, as would most of the clown community. We are totally over the reign of Leo ruddy Leggett, that's for sure."

I nod slowly. I didn't mean to help Leo Leggett cover up his bullying behaviour – but I did. I agreed to the double act; I helped create his nice-guy image.

And I could be the one to tear it down.

CHAPTER 25

What do evil cows say?

Moo ha ha.

In the car, I sit in the back with my headphones on the whole way home, trying to ignore Dad's worried glances in the mirror. He'd hugged me so hard after the show that I'd thought I would explode. When he'd asked me how I was, I just shrugged and put my head down.

Beyond my headphones I can hear Chloe going on about Podge Heg and how funny he is. She doesn't mention Leo Leggett once, which makes me think that she knows too. She and Dad both probably know how awful it was for me. I've never felt so ashamed. If they know then The Regulars will too and Skyla and

Blakemore. Anyone who knows me will have seen that what just happened was not OK.

When I get home, Mum pulls me into a big hug. I can't cope with all the feelings in my body, so I push her off and run upstairs, slamming the door behind me.

Ten minutes later, I hear the landline ringing and Chloe comes up and knocks on my door.

"It's for you, Billy. It's Mr Osho." As she hands me the phone, she whispers, "Just so you know, Leo Leggett is not my favourite comedian any more – you are." Then she skips off downstairs.

Mr Osho must have seen the show. My heart sinks, embarrassment flooding through me. I hadn't even thought about him watching it too.

"Hello," I say quietly, barely able to keep my voice from cracking.

"Billy, I'm so sorry to call you at home, but I saw the show."

There is a pause and I sniff, waiting for him to carry on. My eyes are filling up yet again. When Mr Osho carries on, he sounds furious. More angry than I have ever heard him. Even angrier than when Jimmy Plant called him the worst swear word.

"What that disgrace of a man did to you on that stage is absolutely unforgivable." I can hear him trying to stay calm. "It was bullying in plain sight and I just had to let you know that it is NOT OK."

The sobs start to pour out of me and I can barely speak.

"But everyone l-l-loved him, s-sir. N-N-N-No one seemed to notice that I didn't want him to do it."

"Well, *I* noticed, Billy. I noticed."

I sob into the phone some more, and he waits for me to calm down.

"Th-th-th-thanks, sir."

"You shouldn't have had to go through that, Billy. You can do something about it, you know. Make a complaint to the channel, go to the papers. I will support you one hundred per cent."

"He asked me to tell the n-n-newspapers that he was my hero. B-but he's been bullying me, Mr Osho. I don't think I'm the only one he's done this to either."

"He's got a nerve. I wish there was some way to show the world what kind of person he really is … in a way that people couldn't ignore."

"Me too, sir."

The next day, Blakemore and Skyla show up at my house. They both look furious. I chatted to Skyla a bit last night. She's made me swear on my life not to tell

Blakemore about her mum or the foster house. It feels a bit weird not being able to talk about something so important, but I can't go against my promise, and so, when Blakemore is in the loo, I just whisper, "Are you OK?" and she nods and shushes me. I wish we could talk about her problems rather than mine today. But I know she wants to help.

Blakemore gets back and we sit on my bedroom floor and I tell them everything that happened at the studio and everything Kit said about Leo Leggett. I look up when I finish, and they are both shaking their heads and looking even more angry than when they arrived.

"Kit's right, why would he steal ideas from a kid?" Skyla says, "He's such a weirdo."

"I wanna knock him out," Blakemore says gruffly.

"Unfortunately, Blakemore," I say, "shoving people and g-g-g-giving them wedgies d-d-doesn't work as well in the adult world as it does at school. You're going to have to find other ways of expressing yourself." Then I smile to myself and add, "Although, I would actually love to see you giving Leo Leggett a massive wedgie."

Skyla laughs at this and Blakemore looks even more annoyed.

"He shouldn't get away with it," he says.

"I know, but what can we do?" I say.

Then there is a knock on the door. "PA to Billy Plimpton calling," Dad says in a stupid high-pitched voice and then pops his head round. "Are you all sitting down?" he asks. His face is pink and he's grinning from ear to ear.

"Why are you being weird, Dad?" I ask.

"I've just had a very special email come through, Sir Plimpton. An email that you definitely need to be sitting down to read."

He hands over his phone and I look at the tiny writing. It takes me a while to focus on the words and figure out what it means. After a couple of minutes of silence Skyla can't handle it any more and grabs the phone from me.

"What does it say?" Blakemore huffs as he looks over her shoulder.

Before they can read it I murmur, "I've b-b-b-been invited to perform at the Royal C-C-Cabaret Show in two weeks."

"What?!" Skyla and Blakemore say in unison and Dad repeats it for me.

"Billy here has been asked to perform some comedy for His Majesty the King!"

"And a few million people watching on telly," I add, unsure what on earth to do with this new information.

"They want him on his own as well, not as a double act this time. It would be a chance to be yourself onstage, away from Leo Leggett," Dad says, not trying to hide how he feels about Leo.

"This is massive!" Skyla says.

"Right, I will leave you to have a proper look at the email and have a think about it, Billy. And listen, I know you're not ready to chat to me and Mum about yesterday, but we are here when you are. Even if you decide that you don't want to do this gig, it's pretty amazing to have been asked, isn't it? You are making connections with people, Billy, that's for sure. You just need to figure out how you want to use all this fame, how you can stay in control."

Dad heads off, leaving me to think about it. How am I making connections with people when all they are seeing is a twenty-second clip of me saying my name or being moved around on the telly by Leo Leggett? How on earth does someone decide that I should perform for the royal family when I have barely performed for anyone yet?

Skyla looks up from the phone. "Oh my god, Billy, look at this..." Then she reads out from the email: "*You will be performing alongside some of the best-loved performers of the moment. Acts already confirmed include Energize, Josh Burnside and Leo Leggett, who embody the absolute best of dance, music and comedy. We hope that you will join us in making this a night for the royal family, the country and the whole world to remember and enjoy.*" Skyla pauses for a second, throws the phone down on to the bed and says, "This is it, Billy! This is your chance."

"What?" I ask, not knowing why she's looking so smug.

"You want to expose Leo Leggett as the rat he is, right?"

"Erm…"

"You are on the same show as him in front of millions of people. I would say that's a pretty good opportunity to do it, wouldn't you?"

"Th-Th-That sounds a bit scary to me, Skyla. Performing would already be terrifying enough without attempting to bring down the nation's favourite comedian. Anyway, maybe I need to forget about Leo Leggett. He got me to where I am. M-M-Maybe I should just be grateful and move on."

"NO!" Blakemore shouts. "You have to do something!"

"Since when did you become the mouthpiece of morals?" I shout back.

"Since I realized that standing up for yourself and speaking the truth is tougher than bullying someone. I know I'm still a bit rough, and sometimes I can't stop my anger and stuff and sometimes, well, it just feels fun to mess with the nerds and chuck their bags over the wall but, Billy, the reason I hang around with you is because you taught me all about standing up for yourself." Blakemore pauses to draw breath and then the words keep coming. "I never said it, but seeing you at that talent show telling everyone the truth, well, I've never seen anything like it. I'll never be able to be like that, but you can. You need to stand onstage and tell the world the truth about Leo Leggett, the big bully."

Me and Skyla are open-mouthed. Neither of us has ever heard Blakemore say more than a sentence, so this little speech is a shock to both of us. Everything he says feels right, though. Telling the world the truth is important. Maybe it's more important than how many likes I've got or getting more free stuff. If I don't do something then Leo will keep on bullying people, making them feel ashamed and confused like I did.

Skyla laughs and gives him a round of applause.

"Who are you and what have you done with William Blakemore?"

Blakemore shakes his head and goes red, and when we don't stop looking at him, he throws a teddy at Skyla and tells her to shut up.

Skyla throws the teddy back at him and says, "And he's back!" She laughs and then looks at me. "Seriously, Billy, this is your chance. I think we need to make a plan. Get your notebook out."

CHAPTER 26

I woke up the other day with a puzzled look on my face.

I'd fallen asleep on my jigsaw.

The next day I put the first stage of our plan into action.

I am trembling as I type the words into my phone. I feel sick with nerves. I sit looking at the message, not ready to press send. Not knowing what I am about to start. I know that this is the right thing to do, but that doesn't make it easy. I take a few big breaths and then I do it.

After I have sent the text, I feel like something huge should happen, but there is just the quiet of my bedroom and the faint sound of Chloe singing downstairs. I pace around my room, desperate to hear the beep of a reply – but also terrified.

I need to start working on my material for the show. I have to make the plan work, but I also have to do the best comedy set of my life and I only have a couple of weeks to do it. If it all works I will become the biggest comedian the world has ever seen, and everyone will see Leo Leggett for what he really is.

I sit at my desk but there is no way I can think of anything funny while I am obsessively checking my phone for a reply. An hour later when nothing has come through, I can't take it any more so I decide to go and get Scraggles early and visit Mrs Gibbens.

I need to distract myself from the fact that I may have just made a very powerful enemy. If Leo Leggett wanted to ruin my comedy career for ever then he absolutely could.

"Ooh, my favourite boys, I've got some sausage rolls for you," Mrs Gibbens says when we get there. I think the sausage rolls are mostly for Scraggles, judging by the way he is snaffling them up on the sofa. It's nice to be in her little room – it feels separate to the real world somehow. I go over to the jigsaw which is still sitting on the table.

"You haven't done any of this, Mrs Gibbens!"

"You do it, Billy. I can't be bothered."

As I'm finding pieces of badger, I explain the plan to her. She looks a bit confused and at the end, squints and says, "Will you meet the King, Billy?!" I'm not sure she's followed the whole story about Leo Leggett and Kit.

"I don't think so. He'll be there watching, but I don't think I'll actually meet the royal family."

"What a life we lead, eh?"

Then she looks at Scraggles and offers up another sausage roll. It's nice being with someone who doesn't care about likes or fame or revenge. Someone who spends most of her time thinking about the best treats to feed a dog. It's simple, much simpler than how my life feels at the moment, that's for sure.

As though she can hear my thoughts, Mrs Gibbens turns to me and says, "Are you OK, Billy? You look tired, lovey."

"Yeah," I say. "I've just got a lot to think about. The Royal Cabaret Show is massive, and the Leo Leggett thing is a bit scary and…" I pause, wondering if it's OK to talk about Skyla. She told me not to tell Blakemore, but she never mentioned anyone else and so I continue. "My friend Skyla is at a foster house. Her mum d-d-drinks too much and so she can't look after Skyla for a while. I don't know what to do, or how I can help." I feel even more helpless having said it out loud.

"That poor girl," Mrs Gibbens says and then she adds, "And that poor mother too."

"I don't know why she can't stop drinking," I say, trying not to sound too angry even though that's exactly how I feel whenever I think of Skyla's mum.

"Do you know what addiction is, Billy?" Mrs Gibbens asks.

I nod and stroke Scraggles. "Yeah, it's when you can't stop doing something, even if you know it's bad for you."

"Is there anything you do that you feel a bit like that about? Like you couldn't stop even if you knew you should? We all have things."

"Well, I eat too many sweets," I say and then I feel my phone buzz and it beeps from my pocket. I grab it and check the screen. It's only Dad asking me to get some milk on my way home, nothing to do with the plan.

"What about that thing?" Mrs Gibbens says, pointing at the phone.

"Oh, no, I'm just waiting for a message, that's all."

She smiles and I think about how many times

I look at my phone these days, and how I always know where it is and if it's not in my pocket how I feel a bit naked without it and keep checking the empty space where it should be. How anxious I get when the battery dies and I can't check my likes and comments.

"Yeah, m-m-maybe my phone too," I say, blushing and putting it back in my pocket. "The weird thing is I used to HATE phones. I was scared of th-them ringing! I never took it anywhere, and now I'm scared if I forget it."

"That's what addiction is like; it sneaks up on you and you don't know it's happening." Mrs Gibbens looks suddenly sad, as though she's remembering something. "That poor girl's mum didn't wake up one day and down a whole bottle of wine or whatever she drinks, did she? It would have taken time. She'd have been thinking *what's the harm in one, then two. I can stop any time.* And then one day she can't cope without it. The fear and panic afterwards brings lies, guilt and upset. And then you just do it more."

Her eyes are full of tears.

"I'm sorry, Mrs Gibbens, I didn't mean to make you feel sad."

"Don't worry, Billy. When you are as old as me,

you have experienced so much that anything can set you off." It's hard to believe that Mrs Gibbens has had a life outside The Oaks. I can't imagine her face without the make-up and the wrinkles. I have never even asked her anything about her life – all we ever talk about is the best treats for Scraggles and what's going on with me.

"Do you know someone who was addicted to drinking?" I ask.

"Not drinking, no, but my son was an addict. Drugs. It tore us apart. I didn't see him for twenty years. He's dead now."

"Th-Th-That's terrible, Mrs Gibbens."

"He ended up on the streets."

"Homeless? W-Why could he not live with you?"

"He did, over and over again. Made promises and then broke them. Stole the pictures off the wall once, and then one year took the presents from under the Christmas tree – sold the lot. There was nothing more I could do in the end. It had to be up to him. It's terribly sad, but I've had to come to terms with the fact that it was not my fault. That's what I would tell your friend. It's not her fault."

"Well, I think she knows that. She's only twelve so I don't think anyone would think it was her fault."

"You would be surprised. People who live with addicts often think it's their fault."

I think about what Skyla said about needing to look after her mum, about being there at the right time to make a difference. Maybe Mrs Gibbens is right. Then I feel another buzz. I take the phone from my pocket, then stop. Maybe I'm a bit more addicted to my phone than I thought. As I go to put it back, though, I see the screen.

A response to my message.

LEO LEGGETT: Who are people going to believe? A kid who can't speak or a national treasure? Good luck in the comedy world, kid – you'll be eaten alive.

CHAPTER 27

I fell asleep on my smartphone the other day.

I had downloaded a nap.

Kit calls me back as soon as I text him with the plan. "Hi, Billy. I got your message. I think I can help."

"Great!" I'm relieved. The world won't believe just me – I need some other people on my side. "If y-y-you get in touch with all the comedians you know and send over the pictures, I'll do the rest," I say, starting to feel like a spy or a superhero or a mix of the two.

"You're sure you want to do this, Billy? The Royal Cabaret is such a big deal."

"Yeah," I say. "What he does is not fair."

"Yeah, but he *is* Leo Leggett."

"I d-don't care who he is. If my sister gets more pudding than me, I complain. I started a petition at school once about the Year Tens taking over the m-m-m-music room every lunchtime. I can't exactly ignore this, can I?"

Kit laughs. "Well, I'm with you, Billy. Let's take him down!"

After I hang up, I'm not sure what to do with myself. Putting the plan into action, being recognized in the street and checking my likes seem to have taken up most of my time lately. I've barely even told a joke for the last week. I really need to work on some new material for the Royal Caberet. My slot is before Leo Leggett's so if everything goes to plan, I can show the world how funny I am before it all happens. But first I need to write my set.

I sit down at my desk and decide to try and write some new stuff. Even though Leo Leggett is a bully and a thief, he was right about ditching the joke book jokes and being original. I open a notebook and see the empty page staring back at me. I wish he hadn't stolen the "It's the baby" stuff. Although, I guess if he hadn't stolen it, I might never have even realized it is good material that I could use in a set.

I look back at the blank paper. My mind is just as

blank. I have no idea where to begin. After a period of silence, I check my phone in case anything has come through from Kit. I know it hasn't – I would have heard it beep and buzz – but looking at it distracts me from the reality that I have no idea what to write about.

I remember the talent show and think about my impressions of the teachers. Everyone laughed at them – but that was only because they knew who I was pretending to be.

I look at the phone again. The original clip of me has over five million views now and there are over a thousand comments. I almost know them off by heart. You would think that after a hundred or so reading them would get boring, but it never does. I think about what Mrs Gibbens said about Skyla's mum, how her drinking never gets boring for her either. I put the phone down on the desk. Getting lost on YouTube definitely won't help me write a joke. I keep looking back and forth between the blank paper and the phone, knowing that one is definitely not helping the other.

After ten minutes of it taunting me, tempting me down a wormhole of videos and comments, I go to the wardrobe and bury the phone underneath my jumpers. Two minutes later I hear a beep and can't help myself. It's Blakemore asking about the plan, but once I'm messaging him, I forget completely about needing to write jokes.

An hour later I look up from my phone. I'm still at my desk and the paper is still blank. How will I ever write anything?

I stand up and take the phone down to Mum, who's lounging on the sofa with Auntie Sausage. Auntie Sausage is not really our auntie so I'm not sure why we call her that. The sausage bit is even more confusing. Auntie Sausage has got a baby and so her and Mum have been hanging out talking about babies non-stop for the last eight months. Her baby is called Joy and she never stops screaming. Joy is a pretty bad name for a baby who is always furious. Any time I look at her angry little face and think about her name I want to laugh out loud, so I have stopped looking at her altogether.

The first time she came over I thought the baby was ill or in pain. I had to cover my ears the noise was so horrible. It's no different today: she's squirming and squealing like a pig. I try to ask Mum if she can hide my phone, but the words can't come out over the shrill sound of Joy.

"M-M-M-M…"

Auntie Sausage tries to shush the little squealer, but the sound of shushing just adds to the nightmarish noise. I honestly don't know how my mum just sits and drinks tea and talks through this. I try again.

"C-C-C-C-C..." But I just can't do it. I look at Mum's gigantic tummy and pray that whatever comes out of it does not make this much noise.

I lean over and whisper into Mum's ear, "Don't let me have this till teatime, OK?" and I drop my phone into her hand.

She looks shocked and laughs.

"Happily! Whoever heard of a kid asking their mum to take their phone away, Billy? You are unique, I'll give you that."

Back in my room and away from the screaming, I sit down at my desk. Then I get up again and pace around the room. Then I lie on the bed and stare at the ceiling. My brain keeps darting around – from Leo to Skyla to Kit to babies. I need to get all of these thoughts out of my head and then I can focus.

A list! I need to write a list of all the things in my head. Get them out of there and then they might make some space for jokes. I dash back to the desk and start writing on the blank page. Whatever pops into my head goes on the list.

THOUGHTS THAT POP INTO MY BRAIN
WHEN TRYING TO THINK OF JOKES

1. Mum will give birth to something from a horror film. It will have claws and fangs and make a noise like a screeching train.
2. I wonder if I can see my lips if I push them out in front of my nose.
3. Skyla is being force-fed hot chocolate as I write and needs saving before she pops.
4. My tummy is rumbling. I wonder if there are any crumpets downstairs.
5. Leo Leggett will send people to kill me if I expose him in front of the King. They will wear black balaclavas and burst through my bedroom door.
6. I hate Brussels sprouts so much.
7. Kit is a secret spy for Leo Leggett.
8. Mum might be looking through my phone at this very moment.
9. I wonder if the King can burp on demand.

Looking back at my thoughts and seeing them written on paper is strange. I wonder if everyone's mind comes up with so many random thoughts or am I weird? I literally could carry on writing this list for ever. That's how full my brain is.

When I tune into my thoughts it's like they get louder and I can hear them more clearly. I'm not sure if it helps but at least I have something written down. I wonder if that's why I like writing lists. It gets some of the busyness out of my brain.

I look up at my pinboard with all the stacks of lists fanning out from one another. I never throw a list away. I guess it's a bit like writing a diary or something. I want to keep them all, as they will remind me what I was thinking at the time.

I stand up and carefully unpin all of the rocket-shaped pieces of paper, all of the scraps and bits of notebook until I have a huge pile of lists on the desk in front of me. I go right back to the beginning before my writing wasn't joined up. Even the titles make me smile.

WEIRD THINGS THAT TEACHERS SAY

BEST KNOCK-KNOCK JOKES EVER

WAYS TO MAKE CHLOE JUMP

WORST SMELLS EVER

BEST SMELLS EVER

FAVOURITE CHOCOLATE BARS

As I am looking through them all I start to wonder: is this where my jokes are hiding? Are jokes just the thoughts inside someone's head which are then turned into something funny? Something that other people can either understand – or find so ridiculous that it doesn't matter if they understand or not.

Going through the lists is fun. After an hour I've completely forgotten about the buzzing and beeping of likes and am feeling happier than I have felt in ages.

CHAPTER 28

My mate didn't let me on his boat. He said I was too muscly.

I thought it was a strong friend ship.

"I'm going home!" Skyla is beaming when I open the door. She looks different, so much happier and less tired. I'm only just realizing how awful she must have been feeling now that I can see the difference. It's weird how that happens, isn't it? How you don't notice something that's right in front of you? I feel bad for not noticing.

We have ten minutes before Blakemore gets here and I try to find out as much as I can before he arrives. Skyla still doesn't want anyone else to know.

We take some snacks up to my room and Skyla fills me in.

"Mum has to go to these meeting things every day which help her to not drink, and there is a social worker called Amira who is going to check on us. Mum's agreed to all that, which means I can go home!"

"Are you looking forward to seeing her?" I ask.

"Yeah. She's not drinking, Billy! She's actually getting help. Everything's going to be great this time. It's different. I can feel it."

I don't feel quite as sure, but I smile and nod and tell her how pleased I am anyway.

"I don't care if I never see another hot chocolate and sorry smile again in my life! I'm going home tomorrow!" Then she pauses, her face changes, and she looks at me. "Will you come and help me pack? I don't want to be on my own." Skyla's never asked me to help her with anything before. All of a sudden, she doesn't look like the tough Skyla, she looks lonely and scared.

"Yeah, of course I will!"

Then Blakemore arrives and we focus on the Royal Cabaret Show. I've got rid of most of my joke book jokes and so a lot of the cartoon projections won't make sense any more. I feel a bit bad because Skyla spent so long drawing them, but she doesn't seem to mind.

"I'll just draw some more!" she says, grabbing a pencil. I forgot how much Skyla likes drawing. It's the same as how I feel about comedy. I wonder if she ever has problems filling a blank page or getting distracted by buzzing and beeping. I watch her sketching away.

"Do you want to be a famous artist, Skyla?"

"No!" She laughs as if it's the most ridiculous idea in the world.

"Why not? You love it so much."

"That's exactly why I don't want to be famous for it. Why do you think Banksy doesn't tell anyone who he is?" Banksy is Skyla's hero. He paints things on walls and no one knows his true identity. "If he had to do interviews and photo shoots and was constantly stopped in the street, do you honestly think he would be any happier?"

"I guess not," I say, wondering if my fame has made me any happier. Then I look down at my free trainers – they made me pretty happy. All the other free stuff made me pretty happy too. I think about all the likes and comments and whether the good ones outweigh the bad ones. How I can remember all the horrible things people have said. Maybe I could do without that part of fame.

"It's got to be about the art," Skyla says. "That's the thing I love. As soon as it becomes about me or about money, I would lose that. It's too precious."

"Wow, so d-d-do you think I shouldn't be going on the Royal Cabaret Show? Should I try not to be famous?"

"Well, that's up to you, Billy. Comedy is a bit different, though, because a joke doesn't really exist without an audience. Art exists even if no one has seen it. You've got to find your audience but not let the fame take you over, like Leo Leggett has."

"Talking of stupid Leo Leggett," Blakemore grunts, "I've been working on the video. Any news from Kit?"

"Nothing yet, but he said it might take a while."

"Leo Leggett's career is going down." Then Skyla starts chanting quietly in a sing-song voice, "He's going down, he's going down, he's going down." We all join in until we get louder and louder and are giggling and laughing uncontrollably.

I look at them laughing, and smile at how much Skyla and Blakemore despise Leo Leggett. They used to be obsessed with him. When we were at Field Fest they wanted to see him as much as I did. They didn't need to help me with all this. They didn't even need to believe that he had done anything wrong. They could have just chosen to laugh along with the rest of the world and told me that what he was doing to me was funny, but they didn't. They chose me. I feel so lucky to have them.

The next day I'm round at The Oaks again. Scraggles is crunching up some crispy bacon on Mrs Gibbens's sofa and I'm detaching the pound and putting yet another chocolate orange in my bag, when my phone starts beeping and buzzing wildly. I remember what Mrs Gibbens said about addiction, but I can't help but have a look at what's happening. My Twitter, Instagram and YouTube are all going wild. I scroll through to see what the notifications say.

Stammering boy to perform in front of the King.

Leggett's protégé gets big break.

Will the pressure prove too much for child comic sensation?

The news of who is performing at the Royal Cabaret has been released and it looks like I'm the main topic of conversation. The comments keep on coming as people share the headlines and place bets on how much I will stammer. Some people are saying how much they love me and others are saying they hate me. None of them even know me, I think, but they all have an opinion. It's overwhelming – and amazing. If this gig goes well, then my solo career in comedy will be sorted.

On my way home after dropping Scraggles off, I'm busy thinking about my comedy superpowers and how famous I'm going to become. When I see Skyla's name pop up on my phone, I answer it and immediately start reading out some of the headlines to her.

"Listen to this, Skyla! *Britain's Next Comedy Star? Twelve-year-old Billy Plimpton is to take to the stage in front of the King.*"

Skyla starts to say something, but I feel my phone buzz in my hand and look at the screen flashing up with notifications.

When I bring it back to my ear, she says, "Are you even listening, Billy?"

"Yeah … sorry, no. Insta is blowing up again."

"Do you even know what's happening today?"

"Yes, I do know what's happening, Skyla. I am t-t-taking over the world of comedy and literally everyone is talking about me! You should see the—"

"Are you serious, Billy?" Skyla's voice comes loudly down the phone.

"God, what's wrong with you today? You are so mardy, Skyla. Can't you be happy for me for once?"

"Oh my god!" She sounds furious, but I'm still distracted by the notifications pouring in. "Get a grip, Billy, and think about someone else for a change." Then the line goes dead.

What's wrong with her? But when my phone buzzes again, I instantly forget about Skyla and look at my latest comment:

LOVE LOVE LOVE this boy!

Skyla may not appreciate my genius, but some people clearly do.

And the whole way home I look down at my phone, watching the likes ticking up.

CHAPTER 29

How do you get a baby alien to sleep?

Rocket.

Since I went viral, I've been sneaking my phone into my bedroom at night. Normally Mum and Dad make me put it in the "tech drawer" in the hall when I go to bed, but Mum's got a bit slack since all she can think about is the baby and whether she will be able to heave herself off the sofa.

Under the covers in the darkness, the screen shines out making my face glow, my eyes reflecting all the love that people are offering me online. They also reflect all the hate. Some of the nasty comments are getting worse.

I hope that kid falls off the stage and breaks his precocious little neck.

Talentless. Embarrassing. Go back to school.

I wish I could just delete all the bad ones and only see the good ones. They should make a button for that.

I end up lost in my phone until three a.m., re-reading the posts and refreshing for new comments. I sometimes think about Skyla and why she was so angry with me earlier, but then I get distracted by yet another buzz or beep. When I wake up at seven, I just pick it straight up again and carry on.

"What's wrong with you, Billy?" Dad asks as I yawn into my cereal. "Are you ill?"

"He's been on his phone all night," Chloe snarks over her Rice Krispies.

"Shut up," I snap, putting a box of Weetabix between us.

"Is that true, Billy?" Dad asks.

"Yeah," Chloe continues, loving her new-found power. "It's not been in the drawer all week."

"You are such a rat," I spit, taking her spoon out of her bowl and throwing it on the floor.

"Billy, that's enough! You know we have rules about screens. Look what you've done to yourself; you look a right mess. I will be checking that drawer tonight, young man."

I hate being called young man. I wouldn't get away with calling him "old man" or "ancient man" or even "middle-aged man", would I? So why he has to use my youth against me, I don't know.

I message Skyla after breakfast. It's only nine days until the Royal Cabaret Show and I need to get her final drawings for my set. She doesn't message back, even though I can see by the ticks that she's read it. What have I done? Why is she so cross with me?

There's no way I can go round, I think. She's staying at the foster house – and then it hits me. She's gone home! She is back with her mum, and I completely forgot I was meant to go and help her pack. No wonder she's upset. It's not exactly fair, though – she could have reminded me.

Then I remember her calling me and how I hadn't listened to what she was saying. She did tell me; I just wasn't hearing her. I was too busy obsessing over my fame to notice that she had even bigger stuff going on.

*

Half an hour later I'm standing in front of her door, knocking loudly. When she finally opens it, she scowls.

"Oh, you remembered where I live."

"I'm sorry, Skyla."

"What for?"

"N-N-Not being a very good friend?" I offer hopefully, knowing that it probably isn't enough to earn her forgiveness.

"Why have you not been a good friend, Billy?"

"Because I forgot y-y-y-you were moving back home. B-B-Because I forgot I said I'd help you pack even though I knew it was really important to you. And because I d-d-didn't listen to you."

"Because you were too busy reading your own headlines?"

"Yeah, I know it's bad. It's quite distracting being famous, but that's no excuse. I really am s-sorry, Skyla."

"Just remember what's important, Billy."

"I know," I say, as I feel vibrations from my phone in my pocket. Even I know to leave it and look at it later. "How is it?" I say, gesturing inside.

We leave her house and walk to the little bench in the park while she tells me that her mum has been better than ever. The house is tidy and doesn't smell of sick any more.

"… and Amira the social worker is actually OK. She took me for a milkshake the other day."

She sounds bright and cheerful as she's talking, but there is something else underneath it; I can tell. Maybe fear or worry. I don't ask her about that, though. I smile and tell her how happy I am for her.

"I hope you don't mind, I gave Amira your dad's number. She wanted to know about any support I had … that was before you forgot I was even in foster care!"

"Of course, that's fine. I'll tell him. You know I would do anything for you, Skyla, don't you?" I say as my phone beeps and buzzes from my pocket.

"How about throw that stupid phone away?" she says mockingly.

"Well, almost anything," I say.

When I get home, I see a load of messages have come through from Kit. He's done better than I could have dreamed of.

This is really happening. Now it's all down to me.

CHAPTER 30

Where does the King keep his armies?

Up his sleevies.

There are only five days to go before the Royal Cabaret Show. I'm excited and terrified. I can't quite imagine my life after this is all over. What will things look like? What will the royal family and the whole country think of me?

I could become a legend. The kid who was totally hilarious and made the King laugh harder than he has ever laughed in his life and then showed Leo Leggett up as the villain that he is.

I guess it could go another way. It could all go wrong. I could become a legend for all the wrong reasons. The kid who died on his bum in front of the King and bad-mouthed national treasure Leo Leggett. My comedy dreams really could be over.

I try to hold on to the first version and imagine everyone laughing at all my new jokes and stories. Picture the King's horrified face when Leo is outed as a big bully.

This week I've been offered so much free stuff: go-karting tickets, more clothes, books and even an Xbox with some brand-new games. Everyone wants me to advertise their stuff – it's pretty cool. Leo Leggett must be sent loads of freebies too, bigger and better ones. For a moment, I wonder whether I should just let him get away with it. Keep getting the cool stuff, keep being famous. I'm taking a big risk by making an enemy of him.

My phone pings again. Blakemore has sent over the video for the show. I click on it and I am immediately back on the set of *Morning Live Kidz!* Blakemore has done a great job. He has zoomed in on my eyes and put it into slow motion, with dramatic music playing in the background. It's so clear: the fear in my eyes and the confusion and embarrassment on my face.

It cuts to Leo laughing, moving my head around like a dummy, and then zooms back in on me as I am being flung over his shoulder, focusing in on the tear that falls from my eye. Replaying it again and again. It's perfect. Watching the clip, I feel exactly the same as I did that day and I know just what I need to do. This is more important than being sent free stuff.

Everyone will be able to see Leo Leggett for exactly who he is.

On Tuesday morning, I come downstairs to find Mum bending over, clutching her belly and Dad rubbing her back.

"What's going on?"

"The baby's coming!" Chloe says, looking up from her magazine.

"What?!"

"No, the baby is NOT coming, thank you, Chloe," Dad says. "Mum is just having some tightenings."

"What are 'tightenings'?" I shout. I hate it when grown-ups say things that I clearly have no way of understanding.

"Calm down, Billy, it's fine. They are called Braxton Hicks and it's just Mum's body getting itself ready."

"But it's still three weeks till it's due. Her body doesn't need to 'get ready' yet."

I don't want the stupid baby coming along early.

I will have the rest of my life with the thing; I don't need an extra three weeks of it.

"It's fine," Mum says, straightening up. "I'm just going to go and have a lie-down."

"You can still take me to the Royal Cabaret on Saturday, can't you, Dad?" I say, trying to sound casual while feeling anything but.

"I hope so, Billy. Sometimes babies cause a bit of chaos so it's hard to plan, but I really hope so."

I don't like chaos. In fact, I hate chaos. I like rules and lists and order and planning and knowing that someone is going to take me to the biggest night of my life and not turn around and say, "Sorry, it's the baby."

I can feel the worry and panic rising up and so I decide to focus on the plan and distract myself with how amazing Saturday is going to be.

I've told the Royal Cabaret people that I need tickets for my dad, Blakemore and Skyla. Chloe has been non-stop hassling me about coming, but I lied and told her that I was only allowed four people.

I text Kit and ask him if he wants to come too. He's been so helpful with the plan that I really think he should see it come together in the flesh rather than having to watch it on TV. He replies with a GIF of a dog nodding its head so I email the lady again and give her his details. They're pretty strict about knowing absolutely everything about everyone who is coming. I think it's because of the King. They don't want any randomer turning up. Only Blakemore is allowed backstage and that's because he's doing my tech. Everyone else will have to sit in the audience.

For the rest of the week I work on my set in front of the mirror, and Skyla sends me the final drawings which are as amazing as ever. She's done a cartoon version of me writing a list that goes on and on down to the floor and there is steam coming out of my little cartoon ears.

As I am practising, my phone flashes and rings.

PRIVATE NUMBER

I know who it is immediately. I feel sick. I flip the phone over, but then I panic that he can somehow see me and pick it up.

"H-H-H-H-H—"

"H-H-Howdy, partner," says Leo. Just hearing his voice makes tears prick into my eyes. I hold the phone away from me to try and get him as far as possible from my brain.

"Looking forward to seeing you on Saturday, kid. Are you over your little tantrum now?"

"N-N-N-N—"

"Just wondering if you want to do a bit together for your set. Not sure those terrible jokes of yours will quite cut it on the big stage, you may need a bit of help from your uncle Leo."

"N-N-N-No th-thanks," I manage, as the tears slip down my cheeks.

"Oooooh, well, look at you, all grown up. Don't come crying to me when you die on your arse. Our little ventriloquist act was pretty good, you know. If you change your mind, you know where I am. See you Saturday, Billy. Oh yes, and try not to stammer too much as you don't want to keep His Majesty waiting, do you?"

I take some deep breaths, trying to calm down. Something makes me look at Leo's Twitter feed and the first thing I see makes me gasp.

It's a picture of him and Kit with their arms around each other and huge smiles on their faces. The words underneath read: "So good to be back working with this funny guy."

What? Why is Kit smiling and hugging Leo like that? I don't understand what's happening. Kit is supposed to be helping me. He hates Leo, doesn't he?

I message Skyla and Blakemore and they both message back with the same thing.

It's fine. We don't need him.

Hold your nerve. It's all going to be
fine.

The night before the show, Leo's words are going over and over in my head. Maybe I was wrong about him. Kit has clearly changed his mind about him, so maybe I should too.

But it's not OK to laugh at someone and make fun of something they can't control, is it? It's bullying. He should not be allowed to do that and he definitely should not be the face of an anti-bullying campaign. Why can no one else see that?

Then I remember Mr Osho's phone call after the show. He knew. He saw it all as clearly as I felt it. I have to do this.

I wake up at about five o'clock on Saturday morning. I've had the same dream every night this week: Leo Leggett is chasing me. I wake up when he catches me and I'm sweating and shaking. But last night I turned around and chased him back. I wake up laughing, imagining the shock on his face. Maybe the dream is a good sign that everything is going to go to plan. I hope so.

I need to be at the Royal Cabaret Show three hours before the performance starts. It goes out live on telly and then is repeated again in the evening so we will be able to watch it when we get in. We're setting off at lunchtime to make sure we get there in plenty of time.

I'm in the kitchen, fully dressed with my bag packed and ready to go, finishing off my toast, when Mum and Dad walk in. I know the minute I see them that something is wrong. Dad's face looks tired and worried.

"Right, Billy," he says in the weird quiet calm voice he uses when he's talking about "important" things. "I need you to be grown up now, OK?"

What is he about to say? I look from his face to Mum's to try and get a clue.

"I've got to nip Mum into the hospital for a quick check."

"OK," I say slowly. "We are l-l-l-leaving at twelve, though, right?"

"Well, let's see, Billy."

"What do you mean, let's see? It's not really a 'let's see' situation, Dad. I'm performing in front of the King."

"Yes, and your mum might be giving birth, Billy, so that is kind of more important."

241

"N-N-Not to me!" I shout.

"We will do everything we can, Bill, but I really need to focus on your mum right now. I'm sorry."

"It's not fair!"

"There's no need to panic. Just watch Chloe, and I will ring from the hospital and let you know what's happening."

"I'm sorry, Billy," Mum says and then she screws up her face and sucks her breath in. For a second, I am more worried about her than I am about getting to the show, but then her face goes back to normal and I remember how cross I am.

As they leave the house, Dad looks back and says, "We'll call you in an hour or so. Just don't go anywhere. And watch your sister, OK, Bill?"

I nod, but my brain is already whizzing. Making imaginary lists full of my options. Plans of how to get to the show and how to ditch Chloe. I'm not going to let this stupid baby get in the way of my dreams, that's for sure.

CHAPTER 31

Why are my plans so weak?

Because they never work out.

Chloe knows that she has finally got some power over me. She stands there smirking, hands on her hips.

"I know you're planning to sneak off and do that show of yours. Well, Dad said you have to watch me so I guess that means you'll have to take me with you."

"They'll be back in time," I say, trying to sound confident. "You heard Dad, so don't get your little horsey hopes up."

She scowls at me and swooshes away. I start pacing. What if Dad doesn't get back in time? Hospitals are not pop in and out kind of places. Last time I went to hospital was because I'd fallen off the climbing frame on to my head and vomited. By the time the doctors were ready to see me, it was about four hours later, I'd forgotten why we were even there and I was playing in the soft-play area with some three-year-olds.

I have two hours until I need to leave. Even if the stupid baby isn't coming out, they probably won't make it back in time. I take out my phone. There has to be a way to fix this.

I ring the number on the bottom of the last email I got and speak to a woman. She says that she can change the names on my guest list but one of them has be over eighteen and my named chaperone. She says that she can do all the checks if I give her the names an hour before we arrive.

I ring Skyla but there's nothing: the phone just rings and rings. Then I ring Blakemore and he answers. I explain everything.

"What am I going to do?" I ask.

"I'm coming over," he says and the phone goes dead. I try Skyla again and it just rings out. I must have rung her number fifteen times. Why is she not answering?

*

244

When Blakemore gets here, I'm still pacing. Chloe is watching me, smirking from behind her stupid horsey magazine.

"Not long now, Billy, until you need to leave," she trills. "Shame you can't just leave me here."

I drag Blakemore into my room and slump down on my bed. "What am I going to do?"

"Surely you know a grown-up who can take you?"

"Well, I can't ask any family because they'll tell Mum and Dad."

"What about sir?"

"Who?"

"Mr Osho. You're his favourite."

"Blakemore, you're a genius!"

I find his number in my mum's address book and call it, not even planning what I will say like I normally do. When I hear the calling tone, it sounds different to normal, longer and higher.

"Why does it sound like that?" I whisper, holding my mobile out to Blakemore.

"Abroad," he says and I ring off.

"It's useless. I may as well j-j-just give up."

I sit down on the bed next to Blakemore. I'm completely out of ideas. The strange thing is I'm more upset about letting everyone down and not outing

Leo Leggett as a joke thief and a bully than I am about performing for the world.

A notification beeps on my phone, but it's just a reminder.

Scraggles walk tomorrow.

"I've got it!" I shout and Blakemore nearly jumps out of his pants.

"What?"

"Let's go!" I say and we head out of the door, only to come face to face with Chloe.

"Where are you going, Billy?"

"J-J-Just popping out."

"Shall I tell Dad that you left me here?" she says in a sing-song voice.

"Fine, get your shoes on and come with us, you little rat."

The three of us head out of the door and sprint down the road with only me knowing where we are going.

CHAPTER 32

What do you say to your sister when she's crying?

Are you having a crisis?

We all dash in through the doors of The Oaks. One of the nurses, a new one who I haven't met before, puts her arms out and stops us.

"Whoa whoa whoa, kids. What on earth do you think you are doing, rushing in here like that?"

I try to get my breath back to explain who we're here to see. To explain that I come here all the time and she needs to let me past, but the words are getting stuck and the panic is rising. Luckily my favourite nurse Janice comes to the rescue.

"No Scraggles today, Billy? It's all right, Mags, he's here to see Nora."

I stop for a second. I had no idea what Mrs Gibbens's first name was. I'm so used to calling her Mrs Gibbens that I never even thought to ask.

"Thanks, Janice," I pant and we all stride up the corridor to Mrs Gibbens's/Nora's room.

After we have explained everything, Mrs Gibbens laughs and shakes her head. "Oh, Billy, what an idea. There is nothing I would love more than seeing you onstage and meeting the royal family."

"Well, I'm not sure you would actually meet—" I say, but she carries on.

"But they will never let me out, Billy, not with you lot. I'm like a prisoner in this place. To get out for the day I need to fill in forms and all sorts and I wouldn't be able to be the 'responsible adult' – they treat me like a child."

"But I need you," I say, all of the hope draining out of me. Tears start to prickle my eyes. The realization hits me that this really might be it. I might not make it to the Royal Cabaret Show. I might not get to perform for the King. But worst of all, I won't be able to make things right and fair, not for me but for all the proper comedians who work hard and deserve one tiny per cent of all the attention that Leo Leggett gets. I want to show everyone who he really is.

Mrs Gibbens can see that I am upset and grabs hold of me with her bony fingers and pulls me into a cuddle. Then she whispers into my ear, "There is another option."

"What?" I whisper back, wiping my eyes.

"We just don't tell 'em!"

"Mrs Gibbens, you are the best!"

She looks at me smiling and then says, "So, who is going to drive us there, Billy?"

My heart sinks. Of course Mrs Gibbens can't drive! I look at her expectant face and over to Blakemore and Chloe. Everyone is looking to me for an answer.

"I-I-I-I'll sort it. We will be back in an hour, Mrs G. Be ready."

On the way back to the house I call Kit. It's my only option. He started all of this, I just hope he will be there to finish it. It goes straight to answerphone.

"K-K-Kit, it's Billy. I know that you and Leo made up b-b-b-but I'm still going ahead with the plan. W-Well, if I can get to the show I am. My dad's taken my mum to the hospital so I need someone to drive us there. I think it's important, Kit. The man is a bully. If you can do it then meet us at The Oaks care home in an hour, I'll send the postcode. I will explain everything there. P-P-Please, Kit, I need you."

I hang up. Can I trust him? I don't have much choice.

"Why do we need Mrs Gibbens if Kit's coming?" Chloe says when I put the phone down.

"Kit's only seventeen and I need an adult. Besides, he might not come."

"If he doesn't come then it's over anyway."

"I know that, Chloe!" I hiss. "He'll come; I know he'll come." Although, thinking about the photograph and how happy he and Leo looked together I'm not so sure.

When we get home and open the door, the landline is ringing and I rush in to get it. It must be Dad.

"Hi," I say, trying to act casual and control my breathing.

"Billy, are you guys OK?"

"Yeah, we're fine. Just ch-ch-ch-chillin'," I answer and immediately regret it as it sounds nothing like anything I would ever say.

"Your mum is in labour," he says. "The baby's coming."

"Wow! That's great, so we will just see you later. Good luck!" I say, desperately trying to get him off the phone.

"Listen, I know how disappointed you must be to miss the performance. Can you let them know, or shall I?"

"I will," I squeak. "D-D-Don't worry, Dad."

"That's very mature of you, Billy. I'm sending Auntie Sausage over, but she can't get there for an hour or so. Will you guys be all right until then?"

"No!" I say far too loudly.

"Why, what's the matter?" Dad asks, sounding worried.

"I mean, no need to send Auntie Sausage, we're fine!" Blakemore and Chloe look panicked now too. Then Chloe snatches the phone from me.

"Hi, Dad, I'm just about to start binge-watching every episode of *Free Rein* and Billy is watching YouTube, so we're fine. Is Mum OK?" I look at Chloe, who smirks at me. "Send her our love, Dad. We are set for a few hours here, so tell Auntie Sausage not to worry."

She listens for a minute and then says, "OK. Bye," and puts the phone down.

"Well?" I say.

"He said he would send her over in time to make tea."

"Well, that's no good. What are we going to do?"

"I'll figure it out. You just sort out Mrs Gibbens and everything else."

I try Skyla again, I'm worried she will miss it all but also I know when Skyla doesn't answer that there is usually a reason. I feel a moment of panic for her but I have to keep going with the plan. I email the Royal Cabaret lady all of the new names for the guest list while Blakemore checks that he has the photos and tech stuff for the show.

Half an hour later and we're in the kitchen ready to go. I check Chloe's note, which is sitting on the kitchen table, and I must admit it's pretty good. Maybe I have underestimated my little sister a bit.

Hi Auntie Sausage,

Sorry for the change of plans, but me and Billy are having sleepovers with friends now instead. I am at Aisha's and Billy has gone to Skyla's house. dad thought it would be better as they didn't know how long they would be at the hospital. He tried calling you, but you weren't answering.

Anyway, dad's phone is off as they are on the ward. Sorry to mess you about. See you and Joy soon - it will be so cute for her to meet our new brother or sister!

Lots of love and baby snuggles,

Chloe and Billy

"That's pretty impressive, Chloe," I say, putting it back on the table.

"We are doing persuasive letters at school." She smiles at her handiwork.

"Let's do this!" I say and take a big breath in before we head outside. Just as I get to the end of the drive, I gasp and run back towards the house.

"What are you doing?" Chloe shouts.

"I f-f-f-forgot something," I say. "Back in a minute."

I run upstairs and straight to my desk, grabbing the little bottle of shells and holding it tightly.

"You're not missing this, Granny Bread!"

CHAPTER 33

Knock knock.

Who's there?

Little old lady.

Little old lady who?

I didn't know you could yodel.

We are crouching behind a low wall in front of The Oaks. A man with a dog walks past and stares at us suspiciously.

"I think the crouching is making us look d-dodgy," I say, standing up and edging myself behind a bush. I peek out and can see Mrs Gibbens in the window. For a split second I worry that this could be the worst idea of my life. What if she has another heart attack and I get sent to prison for murder? What if she falls and breaks her hip and I get sent to prison for attempted kidnap? Well, it wouldn't exactly be kidnap, would it? More like old-lady-nap. Before I have time to come up with any more catastrophic what ifs, Blakemore elbows me in the side.

"Where's Kit?" he whispers furiously.

"I don't know."

None of my *what ifs* will matter if we can't even get there, will they? None of this will matter. I won't get to perform and Leo Leggett will continue to be the nation's favourite. He will keep bullying people and stealing material and no one will ever stop him…

As my mind is spiralling, the loud beep of a car, followed by a squeal from Chloe, jolt me from my thoughts. I turn and see Kit grinning at the wheel. He's giving me a thumbs up and I smile and wave back at him.

"Let's get on with it, Billy," Blakemore whispers, looking at his watch.

"OK." I nod. I run over to Kit. "You made it!"

"Of course I made it, Billy, this is massive. I'm so proud of you, buddy!"

"B-B-But what about you and Leo? Aren't you friends again?"

"You mean that picture on Twitter? Don't believe anything you read on Leo Leggett's socials, Billy. That picture was from two years ago! Could you not see my bumfluff moustache and spotty chin?!"

"No, I thought…"

"Nothing is ever what it seems with Leo. He's messing with you, Billy, probably wanted to confuse you. Make sure we never got together and shared our stories. But he's too late. Now, shall we do this?"

I tell Kit the plan. Chloe takes her place near the main doors to keep watch, and Blakemore, Kit and I creep across the front lawn to Mrs Gibbens's window. I have not stood here since she grabbed my face through the window and squeezed my cheeks after Granny Bread died. The memory shocks me and I have to pull myself away from it. That's what happens with Granny Bread memories – they jump out at me when I'm least expecting it. I squeeze my shells tightly.

I imagine what she would say to me if she could see me now. *"Billy Plimpton, you are completely and utterly bonkers and I love you. Go for it, gorgeous boy – show the world what you're made of!"*

Mrs Gibbens opens the window and leans out.

"I've been doing stretches to warm up," she giggles. I climb up and into the flat through the open window. Once I'm inside I move the chair from the little table in the corner to underneath the windowsill.

"Are you sure you want to do this?" I whisper. "I don't want you to get into trouble."

I turn and see her properly for the first time and she looks incredible. Her usual full face of make-up is even more colourful than normal. There are bright pink circles on her powdery cheeks and her lips are a glossy red. Balanced on top of her head is a hat with flowers and fruit attached to it, and her dress is covered in sequins. She is making the whole room sparkle and light up.

"Billy, I am eighty-two years old; I could not give two hoots about getting into trouble."

"OK." I smile. "Let's do it. You look amazing, by the way."

"Well, you've got to make an effort for the royal family!" She winks and then adds, "Now help me out of this window, Billy. There is no way I'm getting up there on my own."

I help Mrs Gibbens slowly get both feet up on to the chair, her frail hands holding tightly on to mine.

"I'm up!" she says. "Who'd have thought I could still climb on to a chair?"

"Well, now we've just got to get you through the window!" I say and I lean out to see if Blakemore and Kit are ready on the other side.

They give me a thumbs up.

It's easier than I thought to lift her through the window. "She's light as a feather," I whisper as I slide her over to the outstretched hands of Blakemore and Kit.

"Wheeeee!" shouts Mrs Gibbens. "I'm flying!" It must look completely ridiculous. An old lady in sequins being flown horizontally out of a ground-floor window.

"Sshhhh!" We all giggle and shush her as she lands gently on the grass outside. A figure passes the window in reception.

"Let's go!" I say as I land next to the others on the grass.

The fifty-metre walk to the car takes for ever with Mrs Gibbens holding tightly on to the arms of Kit and Blakemore. It must be so annoying not to be able to move in the way you want to. I open the car door and wait for her to take the last few steps.

As I'm helping her into the front seat, I hear Chloe,

"Pssst!" and look over to where she's pointing. The new grumpy carer from earlier comes out of the main doors, putting her coat on and looking in her bag. She's heading our way. As the woman approaches, I know I need to do something. I sweep my arms underneath Mrs Gibbens and lift her into the passenger seat.

"My lady," I say, "your carriage awaits," as if she is a Disney princess. She grins as I close the car door just seconds before the carer walks past, still rummaging around in her purse, oblivious to what she has missed.

Kit has the radio playing. On the way to the Royal Cabaret Show, Mrs Gibbens brings out sweets and feeds us all like she does with Scraggles. We are all feeling very excited about breaking her out successfully, but there's still so much to do.

I keep trying Skyla, but when we drive past her house to pick her up the curtains are drawn. I knock and keep calling her phone but she answers neither so I jump back in the car.

"We'll have to go without her," I say, and Kit pulls away. Finally, we head towards London.

After a journey of nervous non-stop chatter and singing, we all go quiet when the landscape changes and the houses build up. Mrs Gibbens had us all singing along to the radio. But now we're looking out at skyscrapers and shopping malls, we want to take it all in.

"Right, we are nearly there," Kit says when we turn into a street with theatre signs and neon lights. At that moment my phone rings and I look down to see Skyla's name pop up on the screen. I think of the darkened windows and the number of missed calls, and a heavy feeling in my gut appears as I answer the phone.

"Where are you, Skyla? W-W-We had to come without you." There is a pause and I hear her breath, fast and jagged.

"Billy, I need you," she whispers, in a voice that I have never heard before.

"What's happened?" I ask.

"They put me in a foster house again, but a different one this time. I'm scared, Billy."

"What about y-y-your mum? I thought she was getting better."

"She ruined it. Like she always does."

"I'm at the theatre. Why is it so bad? Are you being f-f-force-fed hot chocolate again?" I say, trying to make it feel lighter than I know deep down it is.

"I don't want to be in this house. I can't be here

with these strangers." She is properly crying now, her breath still panicky and quick.

I don't know what to do. If I go into the theatre I won't get to her for hours. And she sounds so scared and alone. I look around the car at everyone's concerned faces. They are all here to help me; they are all taking huge risks, putting themselves out just for me.

Maybe it's time that it wasn't all about me. Maybe it's time I put myself out for someone else. I let Skyla down last time when I was too busy thinking about myself. I don't want to be that person again. I want to be a good guy, not like Leo Leggett, all talk and never doing what he promises. Friendship should come before fame. Skyla needs me.

"Send me the address and don't m-m-move. I'm coming," I say, before putting the phone down and turning to the others.

"OK, change of plan," I say. "You are all going in. Blakemore, y-y-you have everything you n-need. You can still execute the L-Leo plan – you know what to do. You don't actually need me. Chloe, you take care of Mrs Gibbens. Mrs Gibbens, enjoy the show. You look incredible; the King will definitely notice you. Kit, I'm sorry but we need to go back."

"What about your gig? It's the biggest audience you will ever get a chance to perform in front of, Billy. You could be huge," he says.

What does that even mean, though, being "huge"? The "hugest" comedian out there is a conman and doesn't seem very happy to me. I have had a glimpse of fame this summer and none of it feels real. I don't feel like a better person or even a better comedian. If anything it's taken me away from real life and sucked me into a world of likes and comments from people who don't matter. People I will never even meet.

Tonight would be more of the same, wanting people who I don't know to love me. Well, I already have people who love me and one of them needs my help. I look back at Kit.

"Some things are more important."

CHAPTER 34

What kind of car does a cowboy drive?

Audi.

"I'm sorry about all the driving, Kit," I say once we've dropped off Chloe, Blakemore and Mrs Gibbens at the theatre.

"Are you joking? I love it! I've only just passed my test so the more driving the better."

"H-How did you get to gigs before?" I ask.

"Trains, lifts – it was a pain in the behind, to be honest. If you want to be a comic then learn to drive. You have to go all over the place. Sometimes gigs are four hours away and most road comics will just do the gig, turn around and go straight home."

"Wow."

"I always think it's more like being a long-distance lorry driver than it is being a comedian. Eight hours driving for twenty minutes onstage. You have to love it, that's for sure."

"I don't know if I do love it any more. I'm not sure I even know what *it* is. I went viral before I had d-d-done a proper gig. It's kind of messed with my head."

"Yeah, I can imagine, mate." We drive on in silence for a bit and I stare out of the window, wondering if I will ever do another gig. I check my phone and send Skyla another message.

There soon x

I remember back to what Mrs Gibbens had told me about her son and write another message.

None of this is your fault, Skyla x

Then I message Blakemore.

How's it going?

Tech sorted. They keep asking where you are. What shall I say?

Tell them I'm on my way.

When we eventually pull up at the address Skyla gave me, I call her.

"We're outside. Shall we knock?" I say to her down the phone.

"No! They won't let me leave, will they? I've only just got here," she whispers.

"Are they that bad?"

"I'm scared, Billy. It smells weird and they've got a massive dog that looked at me funny. I can't stay here, I just can't." She starts sobbing again and I know I need to help her.

I look up at the top windows and ask, "Which r-r-room are you in?"

"I'm at the back of the house in a little box room. The window is too small to get out of – I've tried."

"Oh god, Skyla. Have you rung your social worker?"

"Yes, she's not answering."

"OK. Is your door unlocked?"

"Yes."

"Is there a b-b-back door?"

"Yes."

"OK." I pause for a minute, thinking. "Right.

We will knock on the front door and while they are talking to us, run! The car is out the f-f-front, it's a red VW. We'll knock on in thirty seconds, OK?"

"OK."

I look at Kit. "Are you all right with this?" I ask. "My friend wouldn't do this unless it was really important."

Kit shrugs and his eyes are kind. "Hey, I trust you," he says. "Let's break her out."

Everything goes to plan. The couple answer the door, they are younger than I imagined, and they look a bit suspicious, but Kit is amazing.

"Hello, sir, madam, how are you this evening?"

Behind them stands a drooling dog, who seems friendly enough, but I can see why Skyla was not keen.

Kit carries on. "I wonder if you would like to hear the message of the Lord Jesus today?" I try to keep my face straight as Kit looks up to the sky for divine inspiration. As the couple roll their eyes and try to get rid of us, I see Skyla slipping round the side. I nudge Kit, who says in his most polite voice, "Well, terribly sorry for disturbing you delightful people. We will be off now."

We turn away smirking and walk back to the car, the front door of the house closing firmly behind us.

Skyla is crouching on the back seat. "Drive!" she whispers. "Please get me away from here."

"Where to?" asks Kit.

I look at my watch, realizing that I'm due onstage in an hour. There is no way we can get there in time. I take a big breath in and look at Skyla. It doesn't matter. None of it matters. I made the right choice. I am the person I want to be.

"The Royal Cabaret Show," I say firmly.

"Won't we be too late?" Kit asks.

"We'll miss my set, but we might just make it in time to see Leo Leggett's face when Blakemore takes him down!"

CHAPTER 35

What do you call the King when he's up a ladder?

Your Highness.

An hour and a half later we pull up at the stage door to the Royal Cabaret Show and give our names to the lady who's there.

"Weren't you meant to be onstage already?" she says to me.

"Yes, I'm a little b-bit late."

"Come on, come on," she says, and hurries us through the building, down corridors and up little flights of stairs.

"Now wait here and I will see if you are too late."

As she scurries off, we hear a huge laugh on the

268

other side of the door to our left and Skyla peeks through.

"Leo Leggett has just come on!" she whispers.

We sneak through the door and stand at the side of the audience watching Leo do his falling-down routine. I take out my phone and text Blakemore.

> We are here! You all set?

> Yes. They kicked me out of the tech booth but I snuck back in. Ready 2 go!

I smile and turn back to the stage, eyes scanning the huge audience for Chloe and Mrs Gibbens. That's when I see them. The royal family are on the other side of the room, high up in the royal box, smiling down at Leo Leggett.

Are we about to ruin the King's night out? Maybe he loves Leo Leggett and will be furious and chop off our heads. Too late now.

Leo starts doing some material that leads up to the "It's the baby" catchphrase and when everyone shouts the words, *It's the baby*, Blakemore presses the button and the first projection flashes up behind Leo Leggett.

LEO LEGGETT STOLE THIS JOKE.

The audience laugh, thinking that it's all part of the act. I wonder if they will even notice what all the slides say. Maybe Leo has so much power that they will just keep laughing the whole way through, like they did when he was bullying me.

Leo doesn't notice the screen changing behind him and carries on prancing about onstage. But then the next projections flash up behind him – the texts we sent to each other.

> BILLY PLIMPTON: I am going to tell the world that you stole my joke. "It's the baby" was my list based on my mum and you used it without asking. That's not right.

> LEO LEGGETT: Who are people going to believe? A k-k-kid who can't speak or a national treasure? Good luck in the comedy world, kid – you'll be eaten alive.

There's a bit of nervous laughter when the messages flash up, but the audience goes strangely quiet, and people start muttering to each other. Leo Leggett still hasn't seen the screen behind him and carries on, not quite knowing why his audience is silent. As he struts about, a picture of my "It's the baby" list flashes up behind him, followed by another slide and then another.

LEO LEGGETT HAS DONE THIS TO MANY NEW
COMEDIANS. COMEDIANS THAT SHOULD
BE ON THIS STAGE INSTEAD OF HIM.

LEO LEGGETT IS A JOKE THIEF.

HE IS A JOKE THIEF AND A BULLY.

LOOK CLOSELY AT BILLY'S FACE. DOES
IT LOOK LIKE HE IS ENJOYING HIS
TIME ONSTAGE WITH LEO LEGGETT?

The video starts to play of me being flung around and mocked. As the close-ups pop up, the audience all gasp and Leo turns round to finally see what is showing behind him.

"What's this?" he says, as the final image of the tear falling from my eyes hits the screen. The audience are in shock. Leo tries to smile, but I can tell he's furious. His eyes dart to the tech box where I know Blakemore will be about to press the next button.

AND THAT'S NOT ALL.

A picture of a well-known comedian wearing a red nose and a sad clown face pops up. They are holding a sign saying:

LEO LEGGETT STOLE MY JOKE.

This is followed by a steady stream of pictures of comedians all holding messages. Famous comedians and ones that people have never heard of.

LEO LEGGETT BULLIED ME.

LEO LEGGETT INTIMIDATED ME.

LEO LEGGETT STOLE MY MATERIAL.

Leo Leggett's mouth drops open. He goes to speak but no sound comes out, his mouth opening and closing silently. His face is in shock. Image after image pops up on the screen, ending with a picture of Leo Leggett standing with a huge grin on his face in front of a massive anti-bullying sign.

The audience sit in shocked silence and Leo Leggett coughs and splutters and tries to make it better. "Ha, my colleagues playing a practical joke! In front of His Majesty, as well. I'll get them back!"

There's a long silence.

Then a clear voice rings out from the top, "Go on, Leggett, leg it."

I peer up into the audience to see where it came from, and the King is standing up looking very serious. I will never really know if it was him who shouted it, but I smile to myself, choosing to believe it was.

The audience all join in with a chorus of: "LEGGETT, LEG IT. LEGGETT, LEG IT. LEGGETT, LEG IT." We join in, chanting gleefully. Kit is smiling widely and Skyla is holding my shoulders tightly. Leo looks wildly out into the audience, his comedy façade unravelling. As his eyes travel across the theatre, he spots us. I freeze, my body instantly tensing up.

Kit notices and whispers, "It's OK, Billy. He can't do anything. He has no power any more. Look at them all." I look at the faces of the audience and see their angry eyes. They feel cheated and used, just like I did. They are on my side now. Not laughing along with him.

Leo grabs the microphone and spits his words into it. "Billy Plimpton, you will regret this."

There is venom in his voice. But I refuse to be scared of him any more. He looks so weak all of a sudden. Terrified.

Kit shouts loudly above the noise of the crowd, "If you do anything else to Billy, I think there are a few people who will have something to say about it."

I smile. The audience cheer and Leo throws the microphone to the floor and edges towards the side of the stage, not quite ready to give up his comedy crown.

I can't resist it. Just before he has vanished from sight I call out, "Get in the toilet!"

The audience join me in shouting his catchphrase at him: "GET IN THE TOILET! GET IN THE TOILET!"

When things have calmed down, the comedian who has been introducing all the acts, steps on to the stage and looks exaggeratedly behind him as though there may be more projections about to pop up. Everyone finds this hysterical. After every sentence he says, he cartoonishly checks the screen behind him. *That's what makes a good comedian*, I think to myself – someone who can embrace the chaos. That's what I want to learn. How to get rid of all the lists, rules and plans and be free to play.

When he has finished improvising, he says, "Now, we were supposed to have a new young act on earlier, you might have seen his name pop up somewhere. He gestures behind to the screen. Unfortunately, he could not make it in time for his set. You know how it is being twelve – so many commitments, meetings, Zoom calls, busy busy." The audience laugh at this, and I go red. "But I've just been told that Billy Plimpton may actually have made it and be in the theatre?"

"I'm here!" I shout, before I can even think about it.

The audience all turn to look at me and the cameras swoop in. I give a little wave. The audience all erupt into applause, whistles and cheers. Someone appears with a microphone, places it in my hand and vanishes. The audience start cheering for me to speak. They want to hear what I have to say. It feels so good.

"All right, all right, c-c-c-calm down," I say, and they give another huge laugh. Standing in the audience, after what has just happened, it doesn't feel right to try out my new jokes so I just start talking. Not really knowing what I'm going to say.

"S-S-Seriously, I'm not that funny," I say. More laughter. "You've got to be c-careful who you give that much love and laughter to. Only g-g-g-give it to people who've earned it." Everyone goes quiet now as they start properly listening. "P-P-P-People like Kit and the comedians in the photos. They work so hard. D-Did you know th-they drive for hours to do a twenty-minute gig in some grotty pub for no money just so they can t-t-t-try out some new jokes? I haven't done any of that yet. W-Well, I did it once." I give an exaggerated shudder and the audience laugh. I carry on, seeing if I can get another laugh. "I had to wait in the back bog before I went on. It stank." Another giggle and a few people say "Ahhh". I'm enjoying myself now. "Half the audience left to watch the footy ... all four of them." More laughter. "Two people stayed; they were wearing matching anoraks and smiled at me throughout the whole horrific experience, in the same way that you smile at an ugly baby who you feel sorry for." They really laugh at this. I glance up at the King and he's smiling too.

"Anyway, real comedians do gigs like that all the time. A real comedian like Kit should be on th-that stage instead of me, instead of L-Leo Leggett. He's put the work in and he's funny and kind. All I am is a c-c-c-cute kid with a stammer and some big dreams."

Someone wolf-whistles and a couple of people clap.

"If we make people f-f-f-famous before they're ready, b-b-before they've put the work in, then it's not going to help anyone. If we give people power who are not kind, it creates m-m-m-monsters." The cameras swoop in closer and the audience gets even quieter. They are waiting for me to continue, but a joke book joke pops into my head and before I can stop myself, I'm telling it. "Do m-m-monsters eat popcorn with their fingers?" I pause momentarily, everyone listening, "No, they eat the fingers separately."

There is a mixture of laughter and groaning.

"Leo told me never to tell another j-j-joke book joke." A few people boo when I say his name. "But I love joke books. Who loves a cheesy joke?" Everyone cheers loudly. "Well, you're all grown-ups who should know better, but I'm only twelve." More laughter. "When I'm a proper comedian I will ditch the joke book jokes, but for now I'm a kid so leave me and my cheesy jokes alone!" I look at all the happy, relaxed faces. I'm doing it. This is what I wanted. To be me. To tell people real stuff, to make them laugh, but also to tell them my favourite jokes, because they are part of me too.

"All this t-t-talk of cheese is making me hungry... I Camembert it any longer!" People laugh and groan again. I could keep talking for ever. Not knowing what I am going to say and just seeing where the words take me is exciting. Using everything – jokes, real life and really being here and in the moment – feels amazing.

"Just because I'm making you laugh, though – and I am extremely cute" – I wink and run my fingers through my hair and they laugh and someone whistles again – "d-d- doesn't mean you should let me get away with being mean or rude. We can't ignore the bad stuff just because someone is funny or shiny or rich, can we?"

Everyone claps and whoops at this.

I look at all the faces in the audience smiling back at me. Waiting for me to speak, really listening to everything I have to say. I did the right thing, I think. I told the truth.

I suddenly feel exhausted and want to go home – back to my normal life without famous comedians manhandling me and audiences hanging off my every word.

"When you l-l-l-leave tonight, I want you to do t-t-t-two things: one – look up some of the best comics out there on the circuit, the ones you don't always see on the t-t-telly or going viral on YouTube. The ones who were on the photos."

I gesture to the stage and the images of the comedians start scrolling on the screen.

"Go and see th-them and support them so they don't have to d-do gigs in front of two people in some room above a pub like I did. Secondly, look a bit harder to see the truth because it's not always easy to spot behind fancy clothes, jokes and fame. If you see someone doing something that is not kind, stand up to them. I'm not saying that you need to c-c-c-create chaos at the Royal Cabaret, b-but just speak out in any way you can." I feel Skyla squeeze my shoulder and I know what I need to say. "Anyway, I just want to thank a couple of people for helping me create chaos tonight." I turn to Kit and smile. "KIT PARSONS!"

The audience all clap and cheer as the camera swoops in on him. "The best young comic and long-distance driver you will ever meet." Then I turn to Skyla, who shakes her head, desperate not to be in the spotlight. "SKYLA NORKINS. The best artist and friend I could possibly wish for." Everyone claps again and I see Skyla's illustrations pop up on the screen.

I smile up at the tech box.

"WILLIAM BLAKEMORE!" I point up towards the box and see Blakemore's smiling head pop up. "Best tech and b-b-bodyguard. A man of few words."

I see the fruit and flowers of Mrs Gibbens's hat in the audience. "There are two other p-p-people who helped us g-get here today. One of them wants to meet you so much, Your Majesty, that at the age of eighty-two she climbed out of a window to be here. MRS GIBBENS! And my little sister C-C-CHLOE, who turns out to be more useful than I thought. Thank you for helping." I see Chloe and Mrs Gibbens stand up and Mrs Gibbens waves up at the King, who waves back down at her smiling. I feel the buzz of my phone and see a message from my dad. I grin.

"Anyway, I'd better g-g-go as my mum is actually g-giving birth as I speak and I'm not really meant to b-b-b-be here. I would love to tell you some of my new jokes, but I can't…" I shrug and then add, "It's not me … IT'S THE BABY!"

The audience cheers and all shout back, "IT'S THE BABY!"

CHAPTER 36

What did baby corn say to mummy corn?

Where's pop corn?

Two hours later we pull up at The Oaks and my phone buzzes.

Dad: HOME IN FIVE

"Right, Mrs Gibbens, we need to g-get you through that window in one minute!" I say.

"Billy, you know what, I think I've done enough gymnastics for one night. I think I will just walk through the front door, if that's OK with you."

"Won't they tell you off?" I ask.

"I'll just say I was sleepwalking."

"In that hat?!"

"They all think I've got a screw loose as it is, Billy. Anyway, you'd better hurry up."

I jump out of the car and help her out. When we get to the front doors, she turns and hugs me tight.

"Thank you, Billy, for one of the most exciting nights of my life."

"I'll see you tomorrow with Scraggles."

"Lovely. I've got some chipolatas for him." Then she disappears into the building and when I see all the lights turning on, I dash back to the car. I check my watch and tell Kit to drive.

"They will be back in two minutes!"

None of us say a word as Kit drives. I can feel my heart thudding in my chest. When we pull up outside the house, their car isn't back and I breathe a sigh of relief. Blakemore gets out and heads down the road.

"Ta, Kit. See you back at school, Bill."

I wave. I've barely thought about going back to school. About life getting back to how it was and being a normal kid again. Then I see Mum and Dad's car turn into the street.

"Let's go!" I call to Skyla and Chloe and we scramble out of the car. "K-K-K-Kit, you're the best. See you soon!"

"Bye, Billy. You really did it tonight, mate. See you on the circuit."

Me, Skyla and Chloe all dash through the gate and I fumble in my pockets trying to find the key. I see the lights of the car pulling up. I feel the metal of the key in my hand and I can hear Dad's voice as he gets out, and the sound of the car door slamming shut. I put the key into the lock. I can hear Mum saying something about the baby seat and then hear another door slam shut. They are heading our way.

The front door opens, and we all pour through it and tear our coats off, leaving them on the floor.

"Chloe, go and change into your pyjamas! Skyla, turn the telly on and pretend you have been watching it for ages." They both disappear as the front door opens and Mum, Dad and a tiny, squirming, red-faced grub appear.

"Billy! Meet your baby brother," Mum says, her face tired but beaming.

"It's a b-b-boy?" I ask as I look down into the baby carrier.

"Yup. We need to think of some names," Dad says.

Chloe comes in wearing her pony PJs and immediately starts cooing over the baby and holding its tiny fingers.

Dad leans in. "Sorry you missed your big show, Billy."

"How about Kit for a name?" Chloe says loudly. "Or Leo?" She gives me a wink.

"Ooh, I like Leo!" Mum says.

"No!" we both shout, a little bit too loudly, considering there is a tiny newborn next to us.

"She's joking," I add quietly. "We are not big Leo fans any more, Mum, remember?"

"Oh, I forgot all about that horrible man. Shame, it's a lovely name. Come on, you can both have a cuddle with your new brother on the sofa before bed, eh? Where's Auntie Sausage?"

I quickly grab Chloe's note off the kitchen table and screw it up in my hands behind my back.

"She had to go home. Forgot the baby's nappies or something. She only just left."

Mum nods and Dad is busy fiddling with the straps on the car seat. They barely seem to register what I'm saying. They look so dazed I think we could get away with anything right now. I look at Chloe and give her a thumbs up. She grins back at me.

As we all head into the living room, Skyla stands and gives an awkward smile.

"Congratulations!" she says.

"Oh, yeah," I say. "I f-f-f-forgot to mention. Skyla is staying over." Then I quietly add, "And you might want to check your voicemails; there might be something from a social worker."

"What?" Mum says.

Before she has a proper chance to question it, I say, "You know what, I'm pretty t-tired. I th-think I'm going to head up."

"But don't you want to hear about—"

"Me too," Skyla says quickly, yawning.

"Me three," Chloe adds and we all leave the room as quickly as we can, trying to hold on to our giggles and all the words that we want to say to each other but can't.

Through a crack in the door, we can see Mum and Dad in the living room, snuggled up with the baby, the TV flickering in the background. As they check their phones, they don't notice the opening credits, they don't see the cameras swooping around the faces of the audiences. They don't look up at the screen until they turn the volume up and the voice announces loudly, "Ladies and Gentlemen, welcome to the Royal Cabaret Show!"

I look at the others and we all freeze as we hear the music playing and we know that the compère is about to announce my name on the list of performers. I quickly pop my head round the door and look in.

"There is just one tiny little thing that I forgot to mention…"

One Month Later

I have a new favourite joke.

It's not really a "joke" joke, but it's my new favourite way to make people laugh. Whenever anyone says something that strikes me as funny-sounding, I just repeat them with "You're a…" at the front. It makes even the most boring lessons funny.

The other day Mrs Peat was talking in food tech: "So, you need to roast the veg in the oven beforehand. It adds flavour and no one wants a slimy aubergine in their lasagne."

I leaned over and whispered to Alex, "You're a slimy aubergine."

And he laughed so hard he hit his head on the desk.

At lunch I was helping Matthew with his chemistry homework and he pointed at a "tiny-looking molecule" in his workbook.

I said, "You're a tiny-looking molecule," and he laughed so hard that orange juice came out of his nose.

The great thing is, with this joke, the more you do it and the more unexpected the words are, the funnier it gets. I have as much fun leaning over and whispering things to Alex, Josh and Matthew, making them snort and get told off, as I do onstage.

Shouty Man has left Bannerdale to go and teach in some strict boarding school. Now we have a new history teacher, Miss Back, who makes us dress up in stupid costumes and re-enact things that happened in the past. Last lesson she made me dress up as Joan of Arc and do a French accent. It was beyond embarrassing. Blakemore and Skyla have been calling me Joanie ever since. It's way better than being shouted at, though, and she doesn't mind me drumming on the table and hasn't given any negatives out yet. I also think Miss Back is a brilliant name for a history teacher. I told her this and she smiled and winked at me as she handed me a Roman costume.

Skyla is at home again with her mum now, but she still stays at our house a lot. The social worker talked to Mum and Dad, and they were really upset that they hadn't known how bad things were for her. They did all the checks and said that Skyla could live with us for a bit until her mum got better. Chloe was thrilled and Skyla is so good with the baby; she's better than me. I can't pick him up as he's all floppy and soft.

The baby's called Reggie, but I just call him "the baby". He is occasionally cute and holds on to my finger, which feels nice, but when he squeals I have to leave the room. Luckily he's not quite as much like a squealing pig as baby Joy. Whenever Skyla stays at ours, we're pretty late for school as she's either cuddling the baby or helping Chloe do her hair. I think she feels better knowing that she has us to look after her if her mum gets bad again.

I was offered SO many gigs after the Royal Cabaret Show. My fame went through the roof! I ended up throwing my phone out of the window when all the pings and buzzes got too much. Don't get me wrong, there are bits of fame that I loved. I still get sent the odd freebie, which will never get old. I got a drone the other day! But I don't think I want to be famous any more, not yet anyway. I just want to hang out with my mates and be a "normal" kid for a bit. When I said this to Skyla she laughed and said, "You will never be a 'normal kid', Billy."

All the Skyla stuff and the new baby kind of saved me when Mum and Dad watched the Royal Cabaret Show on telly. They were cross, but I think they were too tired and busy to carry on being angry with me for long. When I explained everything that had happened, I think actually they were pretty proud of me. Even though they said that I had "put my little sister's life in danger, not to mention the life of an elderly pensioner".

I think it's a bit far-fetched saying that going to a comedy show was putting people's lives at risk.

The Regulars are back together, and we are entering the Bannerdale School talent show again this year so we are rehearsing lots. They've said I can tell some jokes in between songs, so it will be like a comedy-jazz set. Mr Osho says that it sounds like his idea of a perfect night out.

More stuff has come out in the newspapers about Leo Leggett today. I had no idea that he had bullied so many people. What happened at the Royal Cabaret Show kind of started a flood of people all coming forward. Even Sal quit. She sent me a massive bunch of flowers and a card.

Billy,

I can't say thank you enough.

Leo has been cruel to me for years and I did nothing, but you have changed everything. I will find a new job where I am treated properly and I hope that Leo realizes that he can't behave that way any more.

You are my new hero.

If you need an assistant one day, you know where I am!

Sal xx

It's kind of scary to think that I might have got cold feet and not gone through with the plan – or that I might not have even made it to the theatre! Then all those people who are telling their stories about Leo might still be trapped and silent. I guess that's how important the truth is. Truth shines the light on to things so you can see them for what they really are. I've shown Leo Leggett up for what he is and his career seems to be over. His sell-out, record-breaking tour has been cancelled and the anti-bullying campaign couldn't get rid of him fast enough!

Fame lets people get away with too much. It made me a worse friend. I only want fame when I am ready for it now and if it's for something real. If it's because I make people laugh so hard that they bang their head on the table or snort orange juice out of their nose then that's fine, but I don't want fame because some stupid superstar stuck ten seconds of me on TikTok.

I'm happy just being the funniest boy at Bannerdale. I don't need to be the funniest boy in the world ... for now.

ACKNOWLEDGEMENTS

What do you say if an onion serves you dinner?

Thanks shallot.

Huge thanks to everyone at Scholastic for being utterly wonderful. Lauren, you are my hero. Sarah, Susila, Gen and Jenny, thanks for all of your editorial help. Andrew Bannecker and Sarah for the fabulous cover and artwork. Harriet, you are a star, and I can't wait to be back working with you and Billy again.

Everyone at Madeleine Milburn, I am so grateful for all of your hard work in getting Billy out there. Chloe, you are the best agent I could have hoped for and Liane-Louise, Georgina, Valentina and all of the international rights team – you are all SO GOOD!! (If you are an author wondering where to send your book and that is the reason you are reading the acknowledgements, send it to Madeleine Milburn, they really are the best.)

To everyone who has ever told me a joke or made me smile: the kids I teach, friends, family, booksellers and people I meet out and about – thank you. You may see one of your jokes in these pages!

To my wonderful family, thanks for inspiring me constantly. Lenny, Cleo, Rob – you make me so incredibly happy.

Lastly to you for reading it! You readers are kind of the most important part, so the biggest of thanks to you.

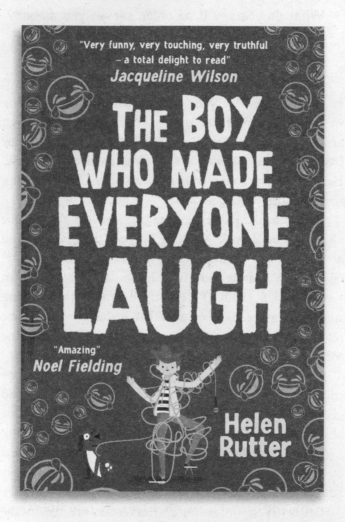

"Very funny, very touching, very truthful
– a total delight to read"
Jacqueline Wilson

THE BOY WHO MADE EVERYONE LAUGH

"Amazing"
Noel Fielding

Helen Rutter

PRAISE FOR
THE BOY WHO MADE EVERYONE LAUGH

"Truly, a heart-tugger of a book. Between the jokes
is an incredibly moving and uplifting portrayal
of one boy's struggle to find his voice. In Billy
Plimpton, Helen Rutter has created a wonderfully
real and inspiring character who reminds us of the
importance of kindness" **Jenny Pearson, bestselling
author of** *The Miraculous Journey of Freddie Yates*

"This book is a great way of showing children how
to be confident by having a sense of humour and
making others laugh" **Baroness Floella Benjamin**

"Who can resist a bit of funny kindness? Not me!"
Liza Tarbuck

"A laugh-out-loud story, the like of which I've never
read before" **Kerry Godliman**

"So funny and joyful" **Rachel Parris**

"This is the book that will make everyone laugh.
Entertaining, endearing, emotional and brimming
with empathy, it's like *Wonder* with one-liners"
Scott Evans, The Reader Teacher